MELISSA

Rosie Rushton lives in Northampton. She took up writing because it gave her a wonderful excuse not to do the dusting and because the word processor was the only thing in the house that didn't answer back. Her three daughters managed to attain adulthood despite having the most embarrassing mother in Northamptonshire. She is passionately interested in family and relationship issues.
In addition to writing teenage fiction and running workshops in schools around the country, Rosie writes a weekly column for her local paper, contributes to a variety of national and local radio stations and writes travel features for national magazines, a somewhat remarkable feat for one who gets lost in a multi-storey carpark.
Her two greatest ambitions are to write children's drama for television and see her first adult novel published before she is too old to look good in the publicity photographs.

Other books by Rosie Rushton, published by Piccadilly Press:

*POPPY

*OLIVIA

*SOPHIE

JUST DON'T MAKE A SCENE, MUM!

I THINK I'LL JUST CURL UP AND DIE

HOW COULD YOU DO THIS TO ME, MUM?

WHERE DO WE GO FROM HERE?

SPEAK FOR YOURSELF

STAYING COOL, SURVIVING SCHOOL

YOU'RE MY BEST FRIEND, I HATE YOU

(* In the same series as *Melissa*)

MELISSA

ROSIE RUSHTON

Piccadilly Press • London

For Mary, who always has the right words

Printed and bound by WBC, Bridgend
for the publishers Piccadilly Press Ltd.,
5 Castle Road, London NW1 8PR

A catalogue record for this book is available from the British Library

ISBNs: 1 85340 550 7 (trade paperback)
1 85340 545 0 (hardback)

Designed by Zena Flax
Cover design by Isobel Smith

CHAPTER ONE
ABSOLUTELY AND POSITIVELY – NO!

"WE ARE DOING **WHAT**?" Melissa Bailey stared open-mouthed at her mother.

"We're moving!" her mother repeated, smiling somewhat nervously at her daughter. "After Easter. We're off to Sussex. I've got this amazing job, the one I mentioned . . ."

Melissa flung her geography folder on to the kitchen table and swung round to face her mother.

"*If* you remember, there was a time when you already *had* a perfectly good job – before you decided to mess up all our lives!" she shouted, brushing a stray strand of auburn hair from her eyes.

"I'm not messing up anyone's life," her mother objected, turning on the tap and filling the kettle. "I'm simply doing what I have to do."

"Oh well, how very nice for you!" stormed Melissa sarcastically, her hazel eyes darkening in her fury. "You can't make us leave London – we've lived here all our lives."

"So perhaps it's time for a change?" volunteered her mother, somewhat unwisely.

"Oh, I get it! Just because you've totally flipped and had some weird mid-life crisis, we're all supposed to fit in, is that it? It's not fair, Mum. What about the rest of us? The boys will go ape."

"Actually," said her mother, dropping tea bags into the pot with rather more energy than the activity required, "they're both rather looking forward to it."

"You mean you've told them? So how come I'm the last to know? I suppose my opinions don't matter!"

Fay Bailey closed her eyes, ran her fingers through her chestnut brown bob and counted to ten. She didn't like to admit, even to herself, that she had taken the coward's way out and told her sons about the forthcoming move before Melissa got home, as a sort of trial run for facing what she knew would be fireworks from her hotheaded daughter.

The boys had been comparatively easy. Ben, at seventeen, cared only about computers and wouldn't notice if he was living on the planet Zog as long as he was hooked up to some Web site, and a moment of uncertainty from eleven-year-old Danny had been easily quashed by the promise of a new bike and some horse-riding lessons. Danny was the sort of child who was never happier than when risking life and limb and had at once appreciated that having large areas of rural Sussex to hurtle around in would give him a great deal more scope for adventure than the rather more restrained confines of North London. Ben and Danny were, to use Ben's phrase, sorted.

But Melissa, her mother knew, was going to be altogether more difficult to appease. She was standing now, hands on hips, tongue sticking rather endearingly through the gap between her front and side teeth, fury written all over her freckled face.

"Well?" She pursed her lips and glared at her mother.

"Of course your opinions matter, darling," sighed Fay. "But you knew how much I wanted this job, an opportunity to really do something . . ."

"You, you, you, that's all you think about!" Melissa tugged at a ginger curl in fury. "I thought you were supposed to be loving and giving and stuff?"

She gulped, close to tears. "And besides, Dad told me that there was no chance of your landing that job."

Fay Bailey raised her eyebrows but wisely chose to say nothing. Hugo was a lovely guy and a very talented architect, but all along he had viewed his wife's new career path as a whim, something she would get out of her system as soon as she realised the hard work involved. Even when she qualified, he had been sure no one would employ her – not at her age, not with her background. Now that someone had, he kept assuring her that he was terribly proud of her and had had total faith in her all the way along. He was trying hard – but she knew by his long silences that he was having trouble adjusting to what would be a massive change in lifestyle for all of them. But at least he was quiet about it; right now she wished she could say the same for her daughter.

"Mum, you can't do this to me! What about my friends?"

"You'll make new ones, darling."

"And Dad's job? You can't expect him to chuck that in just because of you!"

Fay Bailey chewed her lip in the way parents do when they are trying to be hugely calm and reasonable.

"We've talked it all through. He's going to get a studio here in London, and stay up a couple of nights a week. The rest of the time he can work from home."

Melissa opened her mouth but her mother got in first.

"And no, you can't stay with him. Anyway, you'll love it in Mannings Green, and . . ."

"Mannings what?"

"Mannings Green. That's the name of the village. It's just outside Cortlesham." Fay opened the cupboard and began rattling mugs.

Melissa's hazel eyes widened in horror. "Village? I am not – repeat not – living in the country and that is final. All those cowpats and grotty smells. There won't be anything to do. What about shops? And clubs? And . . ."

Her mother smiled. "There are more important things in life, you know."

"Don't you start all that moral stuff with me!" shouted Melissa. "That's what got us into this mess to start with. Well, go where you want, do what you like. But don't expect me to do it with you!"

She yanked open the door, slammed it behind her with all the force she could muster and stormed up the stairs, deliberately clomping the heels of her boots on every stair.

"Melissa, *please* take those boots off!" Her mother's voice echoed up the stairwell after her.

Melissa ignored her and merely stomped even more loudly across the landing to her bedroom, knowing how much it would irritate her mother. She never took her boots off, even at home, unless she absolutely had to. They added three inches to her height and when you are only four foot eleven to begin with, you need all the help you can get.

She stormed into her bedroom and threw herself on to the bed. She wouldn't go. She couldn't go. It wasn't fair. She was a happening person and London was where she belonged. No way was she starting over in some dismal village just to keep her mother happy.

And that was final.

CHAPTER TWO

OH WELL, I SUPPOSE IF I HAVE TO . . .

MELISSA PICKED HER WAY up the uneven garden path and rammed her key into the front door. As usual it refused to budge. Delivering a hefty shove with her left shoulder and a rather vicious kick with her suede-booted right foot, she heaved it open and clattered into the hall.

"Mum! I'm back!"

No response. Melissa sighed. Out again. She couldn't get used to this new way of living. In London, when her mum had been studying at college, they had always had a laugh and a chat when Issy got home. But in the two weeks since moving here, she had been permanently preoccupied with something or someone else. It seemed grossly unfair that in addition to dragging her to this grotty house in a deadly village miles from civilisation, her mother was abandoning her once again to get her own tea after yet another day in the school from hell.

Not, of course, that her mother would see it like that. Not only had she no time to think about Melissa's needs, but she didn't have a clue about what life was really like at Furze Grange Upper School.

"I know it's a big change for you, sweetheart, but look on it as a challenge, a great adventure," her mother had said soothingly the previous day when Melissa had listed all the ways in which Furze Grange was not a patch on her old school. "That's how I'm viewing all this."

Which was easy for her to say, with everyone in the village bowing and scraping and bringing sponge cakes and home-made soup and sucking up to her right, left and centre, like she was some gift from God. She should try dealing with the likes of Ellie Balfour and Tara Kimble every day, then she might realise just how difficult life could be out in the real world.

It wasn't that people were being unfriendly exactly

– indeed, several of the girls in year ten had become very attentive when they discovered that Melissa had a seventeen-year-old brother, and no, he didn't have a girlfriend, and yes, he was OK-looking. But every time the subject got round to parents, their reaction was always the same.

"My dad's an architect," she had told them on the first day of term when the inevitable quizzing started.

"What about your mum?" Ellie Balfour had chirped up, inspecting a broken fingernail with the disgust of one who knows that digital perfection counts for a lot more than good grades.

Melissa had taken a deep breath. "She's the new curate at St Peter's. In Mannings Green," she had gabbled.

"The what?" Ellie had looked puzzled.

"You mean, your mother's a *priest*?" Tara Kimble had interjected incredulously. "Really?"

Melissa had nodded in a resigned way.

"Poor you," commented Hannah Rolfe, her chubby face puckering in a sympathetic frown. "Do you have to pray all day and stuff?"

Melissa had laughed, self-consciously running her fingers through her hair. "Of course not," she said. "She's just like any other mum, except she works in a church instead of an office."

She could tell from their briefly-exchanged glances that they didn't believe her. She had known they wouldn't. Her mother had assured her that if she put it like that, no one would think twice about it – but then her mother, despite having a posh degree and writing sermons full of long words, could be remarkably stupid.

"I bet it's dire in your house," Tara had remarked, pulling the ring off a can of cola. "All that holiness."

"It's not like that, honestly," Issy had assured her. "We're just normal – well, I am, anyway. I'm not so sure about the boys."

"Talking of boys," Ellie had added, crossing her legs and tossing her head provocatively, "I suppose you're not allowed boyfriends?"

"Of course I am!" expostulated Melissa who, much to her regret, had never really had the chance to put the theory to the test.

"So have you got one?"

"Well, no, not right now, but . . ."

"That's what I thought," smirked Ellie, eyeing her up and down. "You only look about twelve."

That, thought Melissa now, hurling her schoolbag on the bottom stair and throwing her jacket over the banisters, just about did it. Being so small was bad enough – if she got a boyfriend she probably would not be able to reach to kiss him, which had always been a worry – but she had always felt she did rather compensate for it with her own brand of wacky style. Or at least, she had done at her old school.

Lord Tennyson High had been a forward-looking establishment, whose head believed that pupils should not be subjected to uniform but should express their individuality in the way they dressed, a concept which Melissa had taken devoutly to heart. Ever since it had become apparent that any amount of visits to Fringe Affairs would not prevent her unruly mass of ginger curls from living a life of their own, and since her cash-conscious father had declined to offer her cosmetic surgery to remove her freckles, she had decided to do what the Image Maker pages of *Heaven Sent* magazine instructed, and turn negatives into positives.

She covered her detested red hair with a selection of funky hats that she collected from street markets – velvet cloches, baseball caps, tweed berets, even a really wicked brown trilby. She hung the zaniest earrings she could find from the five assorted holes in her lobes – making sure, of course, that none of them ever matched. Every meticulously varnished finger sported a really cool ring and she overcame the problem of the gap between her front and side teeth by sticking her tongue in the hole when she grinned. By dressing as wackily as possible she reckoned people stopped noticing how little there was of her. And in London it had worked. But now the combined forces of her inconsiderate mother and the outmoded rules of Furze Grange school were threatening to relegate her to the status of number one anorak.

You would have thought, mused Melissa, throwing open the sitting-room door and cringing yet again at the onslaught of rose-pink floral wallpaper, that a mother would have wanted to do all in her power to make life easier for a daughter who was doomed to wear a maroon blazer with gold braid and a hideous striped tie. It wasn't as if Fay was frumpy; there had already been some raised eyebrows in the village when she had appeared at a PCC meeting in stonewashed jeans and cowboy boots. Yet, despite having a blazing row in the middle of Marks and Spencer, Fay Bailey had refused to buy Issy this really fetching charcoal grey miniskirt with a suede belt and side slit and instead had scooped up two of the foulest, most shapeless regulation school skirts ever designed.

"It says 'grey skirt'," Issy had insisted, stabbing a blue-varnished fingernail at the uniform list. "It doesn't say what kind."

"That," her mother had retorted, removing the miniskirt from her daughter's clutches, "is not a skirt. It's a hairband."

"It'll show off my legs," pleaded Melissa, who considered her lower limbs to be the only acceptable part of her entire anatomy.

"That is precisely," declared her mother, "what I am worried about."

"Priests," said Melissa pointedly, "are meant to be hugely tolerant."

"Mothers, however, are not. I'm not having you breaking school rules before you even get there."

It was that sort of attitude, thought Melissa now, slamming the sitting-room door and clomping down the draughty hallway towards the kitchen, that gave people like Ellie all the ammunition they needed. Ellie was tall and reed-like, and she had definitely doctored her school skirt, since it moulded itself alluringly round her hips and stopped a good ten centimetres above her knees, while Melissa's own shapeless garment made her look like a rather cheap lampshade. Add to that the fact that Furze Grange didn't allow hats in school or any form of jewellery except 'small, tasteful studs', and it was hardly surprising that people thought she looked like a kid. Well she wasn't going to put up with it a moment longer. She had worked out what needed to be done and now it was down to her mother to see that it got sorted.

"Mum?" Melissa peered hopefully round the kitchen door. The room was silent apart from the steadily dripping tap, which her father had been promising to fix since the weekend they moved in. Issy opened the fridge and sighed. One tub of cottage cheese (and not even the kind with prawns in), a small egg and a carton of milk. It simply wasn't good enough; how could she be expected to face two hours of mind-stretching homework without a substantial intake of carbohydrate? She glanced along the counter tops in the hope of finding a note from her mother, but all she discovered was a shrivelled piece of carrot and a few biscuit crumbs. She licked her index finger and stabbed them up into her mouth. Desperate times led to desperate measures.

She had just poured a glass of milk when she heard footsteps clattering down the still uncarpeted stairs.

"Mum?" She opened the kitchen door and looked up hopefully.

Her father, carrying a tan overnight bag in one hand and pulling at the neck of his black polo shirt with the other, grinned down at her, his pale green eyes twinkling with pleasure at seeing his daughter. It was, Melissa thought distractedly, unfair that the gap in *his* teeth gave him an air of the artistic eccentric, while her own made her resemble a dippy cartoon character from Trouble TV.

"She had a meeting with Donald – the vicar," Hugo Bailey announced, jumping down the final three stairs, dumping his bag on the floor and giving her a hug. "And then she was off to the supermarket to lay in supplies."

"Oh good!" retorted Melissa. "Nice to think she can fit in our needs once in a while."

"Oh come on, Issy!" her father exclaimed, a frown creasing his high forehead. "I know it's hard but you mustn't take that attitude, darling. We've all got to rally round and support Mum in this venture – the world needs more people like her."

Melissa nodded reluctantly. "I know," she sighed. "But I just don't understand – I mean, if she'd wanted to be a curate, why didn't she do it years ago? Then she could have been a bishop by now and I could live in a decent house instead of this dump."

Her father shrugged and smoothed an errant strand of sandy hair back into place. "You know your mother," he said. "That part-time job at the publishers was all right, but she always felt she was meant to do something more. Putting something back, she called it. She told me that she tried to ignore it but the feeling wouldn't go away. And well, you know the rest."

"The rest," said Melissa wryly, "being a dead village, a crumbling house and no friends." To her annoyance, she felt her eyes filling with tears.

Her father stretched out his hand and tousled her hair. "It'll get better, Issy," he said comfortingly. "It's early days yet for all of us. Actually, I've got some brill ideas for this place. Want a look?"

Melissa nodded eagerly. Although her father was known in architectural circles for his steel and glass office complexes, he was a whizz at interior design and Melissa's old bedroom in London had been the envy of her friends, with its mirrored wall and wacky pyramid lights.

"Come through." Hugo opened the door to his study, still full of unopened packing cases, and gestured to his drawing board, on which a series of sketches lay haphazardly strewn.

"I thought we could knock the wall between the sitting-room and dining-room into a sort of porthole with steps – arches have been done to death – then strip the floors and doors and unblock the fireplace and have a sandblasted stone hearth and surround. What do you think?"

"Great!" Melissa enthused. "And can we have a second bathroom?"

The bathroom was a particular source of irritation to her. Not only was the shower so ancient that all you got was a lukewarm trickle, but with five people in the family she never had time to do the things she needed. Even now she sported one defuzzed leg and one hairy one, because Ben wanted to wash his hair before college and her mother, in one of her more pompous frames of mind, had told her that vanity would be her downfall.

"I doubt it – there isn't the space," said her father. "But I'll work on it."

Which meant, thought Issy, that it was as good as done because her father could make anything happen when he put his mind to it.

There was the toot of a car horn from outside the window and Hugo glanced in surprise at his watch. "That'll be the taxi – must dash, or I'll miss the train."

He hurried out into the hall and Melissa followed him, frowning. "What train?"

"I'm going up to London for a couple of nights," her father informed her. "Got a dinner meeting tonight and some meetings to go to – and I thought I might take in that Degas exhibition."

"Lucky you!" said Melissa. "Two days in civilisation."

Her dad nodded eagerly and then stopped, as if unsure that he had given the right response.

Melissa wasn't fooled. "You hate it here too, don't you, Dad?"

Her father dropped his eyes and bit his lip.

"'Course not," he said brightly, still not looking at her. "All this peace and fresh air? Can't wait to get back."

He didn't, thought Issy, sound convinced.

He slung his bag on his shoulder and gave her a kiss on the top of her head. "Bye, baby bunting, I'll call . . ."

"Don't call me that!" Melissa snapped.

Her father looked at her in astonishment and held up his hands in mock surrender. "Sorry! Force of habit. I've always called you that – you never used to mind."

"Well, I do now!" She needed reminders about her failure to grow like she needed a hole in the head.

The taxi horn tooted once more, rather more insistently.

"OK, see you Friday night!" Her father did battle with the reluctant front door, which finally yielded to his not-inconsiderable strength. "Have fun!"

"Fat chance," Issy muttered under her breath as the door slammed shut. Fun and Mannings Green hardly went together. In fact, she would probably never have any fun ever again. All that lay ahead of her that evening was an essay on photosynthesis and four totally impossible maths questions. She wished she could be like her father and shoot back to London whenever the mood took her.

She grabbed her schoolbag and clomped upstairs, wondering what on earth possessed the previous occupant to put seashell wallpaper on the staircase. Perhaps clergy people were too taken up with higher thoughts to notice grot when they saw it.

As she reached the landing, her bedroom door opened and to her astonishment a chubby boy with a very unfortunate haircut crashed out.

"I'll get a box or something . . . oh, hi!" He pushed past her and clattered downstairs.

"What on earth . . . ?" Melissa marched into her bedroom to find two pairs of legs sticking out from under her bed.

"Danny! How dare you come into my room! What do you think you are doing?"

One pair of the legs wriggled backwards, followed by the skinny torso of her younger brother, covered in carpet fluff and looking somewhat flushed.

"Oh, it's you," he said in a thoroughly unconcerned manner. "I've lost Humphrey."

Melissa's eyes widened. "And who, or what, is Humphrey?" she demanded.

The other body had by now extricated itself from beneath the bed and stood up. A spotty boy with round glasses and an earnest expression grinned down at her. Life was bad when eleven-year-olds were taller than you were.

"He's a white rat," said the boy helpfully. "He was mine but I've got five and Danny hasn't even got one pet so . . ."

"A *rat*?" screeched Melissa. "And it's in my room?" She backed towards the door.

"No, sadly, it appears he's not," sighed Danny. "I guess we'd better try Mum and Dad's room."

"Just find it!" shouted Melissa with a shudder.

"And get rid of it!"

Danny looked offended. "Him, not it," he retorted. "And I'm keeping him."

"I doubt it very much," responded Melissa. "Mum would go ballistic."

"She can't," said Danny smugly. "Now she's a proper curate she has to live in love and peace with all. It's one of the rules."

"Rules," said Melissa dryly, "can be broken."

Danny stuck his tongue out at her. "Well, I heard Mum telling Dad that it didn't take much to keep me happy and she wished the same could be said for you and it was time you made an effort and stopped moping around, so there!"

"Some of us," retorted Melissa, "need more than a dirty rat to make our lives . . ."

"Hey, Danny, I think I've found him!" a high-pitched voice echoed up the stairs. "Out here! Quick!" At which the two boys hurtled out of the room and galloped downstairs, shrieking at the tops of their voices.

"Oh go back to kindergarten, pea brain!" Melissa shouted, slamming her door and pulling her school sweater over her head. That was all she needed, a kid brother with a rat for company. Except that it wasn't just the rodent; it wasn't even the grossly unfair comments made by her mother. What really got to her was the fact that Danny, who was loud and scruffy and a total pain, had managed to find two real mates within the first few days at his new school while she, who had been voted class captain twice at Lord Tennyson, hadn't got anyone. She tagged along with Tara and Ellie and they tolerated her, and a couple of the boys had eyed her with interest once or twice, but she hadn't met anyone she really clicked with, no one with whom she could imagine sharing her innermost thoughts and feelings. And certainly no one who wasn't going to be put off by being friends with a curate's kid.

She threw her hated school skirt on to the floor and stepped into a pair of stretch jeans. Slumping on the bed, she flicked open her maths folder and glanced nervously at the first question. It might as well have been written in Japanese for all the sense it made to her. She knew she wasn't clever but at Lord Tennyson that hadn't seemed to matter – she was the ringleader of her set, the one with the cool ideas, who was just charming enough to the teachers to keep them sweet, and just wicked enough to earn her the reputation among her friends of being a real laugh. At this new school, they were all judging her by what her mother did and it wasn't fair. And what was more, she wasn't going to put up with it any longer.

She simply had to prove that she was really sussed and sassy, and nothing like the goody-goody that Ellie was telling everyone she must be. And the first way to do that was to get her appearance sorted. Never mind mothers, never mind school rules; from now on, Furze Grange was going to see a totally new Melissa Bailey.

And if her mother didn't like it, that was just too bad.

Half an hour later, she thought she had it sorted. From the mountain of clothes which she had flung on to her bed she had pulled out a dead glam, V-necked vest top and a tailored white shirt, a pair of grey diamond pattern tights shot through with silver Lurex thread and her wicked knee-high patent boots. Standing in front of her mirror, she peered critically at her reflection. With the top two buttons of the shirt left undone and the vest top showing through, she reckoned she looked pretty sophisticated, and there was just enough of the tights showing above the top of the boots to be rebellious without, hopefully, earning detention for what Mrs Fisher called "non-observance of the dress code". She pulled her mass of hair tightly back off her face and screwed it into a knot held in place by a fake tortoiseshell comb. Very suave. The only thing ruining the total look was the naff lampshade skirt.

Melissa opened her dressing-table drawer, took out a pair of nail scissors and slid the open blade across the stitching along the hem. She then lay the skirt on the floor and trod heavily on the bottom a few times. Standing back, she surveyed the resulting mud patches with satisfaction. All she had to do now was find the box of pins and she was in business.

She threw on her jeans and her black chenille sweater and was halfway downstairs in search of her mother's workbox when the back door slammed. At last! She was home, hopefully with large quantities of food and a rather more open mind than usual. Melissa jumped down the last two steps and hurried along the hall, fixing a suitably worried expression on her face.

"Hi, Mum! Good day? Look, I'm really sorry but I fell over and . . . oh!"

Standing on the doormat, removing a voluminous blue plastic mac and an astonishing scarlet rainhat, was an exceedingly thin woman with skin like corrugated paper and several layers of bright blue eyeshadow that appeared to have been applied with a palette knife.

"Oh hello, dear," said the apparition, stuffing the mac into a huge shopping bag and revealing a bright red sweater adorned with a crocheted poodle, and a pair of trousers that would not have been out of place on Rupert Bear. "You'll be Melissa, very nice to meet you. Mrs Curate said you'd be in. Isn't she back yet? Well, no, I suppose, poor dear, she's still ministering, God be praised. Such a lovely lady and you've got her eyes, lucky girl. Now, where are the cloths?"

Melissa swallowed. "Excuse me?"

The woman slapped a bony hand on her arm. "There I go, yattering on, and you not knowing whether I'm the Queen of Sheba or an alien from Mars."

Looking at her, Melissa was tempted to opt for the second alternative.

"Connie, dear – Connie Jupp. I sort out the vicar."

She said this with the dignity of one who has just been instrumental in bringing about a lasting peace in Northern Ireland.

"I . . ." began Melissa, but Connie was in full flood.

"And I said to Vicar, we can't have Mrs Curate rushed off her feet getting to grips with St Peter's and the old folk and all, and then having to do for her little tribe, and me sat at home in the afternoons twiddling my thumbs, and Vicar said, 'You are so right, Connie but then aren't you always?' Vicar gives praise where praise is due, I'll give him that. I did for the last curate but he left under a cloud, dear. Enough said. So now, dear, if you'll just point me in the direction of the cloths."

Light finally dawned. "So you've come to clean?" Melissa exclaimed.

Connie drew herself up to her full height which, Melissa noticed with some satisfaction, was still two inches shorter than her own. "Housekeep, I prefer to call it, dear," she said. "Three till six, Mondays, Wednesdays and Fridays I thought. Well, I'm late today what with my feet, but that's the arrangement, and very pleased your mother was when Vicar told her. 'Connie's the best,' he said. 'She can do it all,' he said. 'Clean, iron, shop, mend . . .' "

"Mend?" Melissa's brain went immediately on to red alert.

"Handy with a needle, even though I say it as

shouldn't," nodded Connie proudly. "My mother was always one to get us girls ready for whatever life threw at us. 'Connie,' she would say, 'if you can stitch a fine seam, you won't go far wrong.' "

Melissa set her features into her charming-yet-rather-anxious expression and nibbled her lip. "I wonder – could I possibly ask your advice?" she said meekly.

" 'Course, dear – what's up?"

Melissa fluttered her eyelashes. "I fell over on the way home from school and ripped the hem of my skirt. Only I'm awful at sewing and Mum is so busy that I don't want to bother her."

Besides which, she will see through me in ten seconds, she added silently.

"Oh, I can put that to rights in no time," declared Connie. "Hand it over."

Melissa swallowed. "Look, I'll just put a few pins in, to show you what length it has to be, OK? Oh, and the cloths are under the sink."

"Right you are, my lovely." Connie pulled open the under-sink cupboard and surveyed the motley assortment of detergents and dusters with the air of one who has been used to better things. "Just pop your skirt on top of my bag when you're ready and I'll do it before I go."

Yes! thought Melissa, silently punching the air in triumph. She found the pins and turned the hem up eight centimetres higher than before. She held it in front of her and smiled to herself. Better. Much, much better.

"Connie – you won't say anything to Mum, will you? About the skirt?"

Connie eyed her quizzically. "I'll just mend it and hold my tongue," she said with a grin. "The rest is up to you. Now if you don't mind, I'm going to start on my downstairs furniture."

Melissa looked at her. Connie winked, and marched, bucket in hand, out of the kitchen. Melissa was about to call after her when there was a squealing of brakes outside, a scrunching of gravel and an ear-piercing scream.

Melissa yanked open the back door in time to see her mother careering through the side gate at high speed, hotly pursued by Danny and his friends.

"Just get that thing away from me!"

"It's OK, Mum, it's all right, you didn't hurt him!" Danny panted.

Melissa's mum hurled a couple of loaded carrier bags on the floor and looked round in horror.

"You stopped in time," said the spotty boy. "That was cool."

"Are you telling me," Fay Bailey said in the breathless tones of one who is fighting hysteria, "that someone actually owns that – that *thing*?"

"He's not a thing, he's a white rat, and he's called Humphrey and Sam gave him to me only I haven't got a cage yet and that's why he keeps getting free."

"He was running all over the house an hour ago,"

added Melissa, for good measure. "It's so unhygienic."

"That," interjected the spiky-haired boy loftily, "is actually untrue and is a very common prejudice, especially among women. My father says."

Melissa glowered at him.

"Luke's dad is a vet," explained Danny. "He says that getting close to the animal kingdom is an essential part of a child's development."

"Does he indeed?" said Fay in a somewhat un-curate-like manner. "How interesting. Well, perhaps Luke and Sam would like to go now, and 'get close' to that thing somewhere else."

"But Mum . . ." began Danny.

"But nothing. Take it away. Now!"

Luke and Sam hesitated, caught sight of the expression in Mrs Bailey's eyes and went, Luke clutching Humphrey, nose twitching, to his none-too-clean sweatshirt.

Danny stood in the middle of the kitchen floor, hands on hips and glared at his mother. "You can't do that, you can't stop me having Humphrey," he said in the tones of one who knew he had the upper hand.

"Why not?"

"Because Luke's dad goes to St Peter's and he'll tell everyone that you broke the rules. You're supposed to love all God's creatures and he'll say that you don't love Humphrey and you'll be exposed as a fraud."

"I'll chance it," said his mother, trying not to smile.

"Oh stop being ridiculous, Danny!" interjected Melissa. "Leave Mum alone. She's had a tough day."

Danny pouted, stuck his tongue out and stomped out of the room.

Fay eyed her daughter in surprise. White rats and stroppy little boys were par for the course, but Issy expressing concern for her mother's emotional wellbeing was little short of a miracle.

She was about to enquire further into this sudden upsurge of solicitousness when the kitchen door opened and Connie, flushed and smelling of lavender furniture polish, poked her head round.

"Oh, Mrs Curate, you're back. Lovely. And that must be little Daniel on the stairs, bless him, the cherub."

Melissa decided that either Connie was having them on or her powers of appraisal were sadly lacking.

"Now look, my dear, I've done your downstairs and I'd like to start on the bedrooms, only I've forgot Barnaby and if he doesn't get his tea he'll create something terrible and I wouldn't want you upset like that."

"Barnaby?" smiled Fay, head to one side in concerned-and-deeply-interested mode.

"Yes, I've tied him up so there won't be any trouble but he frets, you know, well, they do, that sort, don't you find?"

Melissa and her mother exchanged glances.

"I'm sorry, but just who is tied up where?" asked Fay.

Connie tapped her hand to her forehead. "Silly me," she said, "you won't know about Barnaby. He's a dog. Well, hardly more than an overgrown puppy really. Belonged to old Mr Forrest but he went to stay with his daughter – well, he had to with his hips – and he was in a right state about leaving the dog and asked me to keep an eye till he got back – but of course we all knew he wouldn't come back – not with those hips – and now I'm tied. To the lamppost."

It took a moment for Melissa to deduce that this latter reference was to Barnaby and not Connie Jupp.

"So if I could just take him some water, I've got his biscuits in my bag, he likes the oval ones, you know, with the added . . ."

"Yes, yes of course," interrupted Melissa's mother speedily, feeling too exhausted to cope with yet another of Connie's bouts of verbal diarrhoea.

"I'll do it," said Melissa eagerly. "Then you can get on."

The sooner Connie finished messing about with dusters the sooner her skirt would be rendered fit to wear.

"Oh, you are a duck," said Connie. "I'll go and make a start on my grate, then."

She departed, tunelessly humming something about doggies in windows.

"What about homework?" demanded Melissa's mother, who shared the universal parental attitude that the whole of life, including expiring dogs, had to be put on hold until assignments were finished.

"Done it," Melissa lied.

"Almost," she added, weakening under her mother's laser-like gaze and, grabbing the biscuits and a bowl marked 'Dog' from Connie's bag, she sped out of the door.

"Hi, Barnaby!"

Two huge, soulful eyes opened wearily and gazed at her.

"Look, I've got biscuits!"

A rather mangy tail began thumping rhythmically up and down on the pavement.

"And water!"

A long, unco-ordinated tongue lapped ecstatically, sending droplets of water all over Melissa's boots.

She peered at him. "What are you exactly, I wonder?" she said out loud.

Barnaby gobbled another mouthful of biscuit and looked at her, as if asking precisely the same question about her.

She put her head to one side and eyed him quizzically.

He did the same.

"Sort of wolfhound mixed with Labrador with sheepdog connections," she mused, ruffling his sandy-and-black-speckled coat.

Barnaby grinned a soppy, doggy grin and sat in his water bowl.

"Stupid dog!" giggled Melissa. She dropped down on to one knee and a ridiculously huge head flopped itself on to her other knee and dribbled unself-consciously down her trousers.

"Melissa! Homework!" Her mother's voice rang out from an upstairs window.

Reluctantly Issy stood up. "Got to go," she told Barnaby. "Maths and photosynthesis. You don't know how lucky you are to be a dog."

She turned. A huge paw patted her calf and a little whimper tugged at her heart-strings.

She eyed him. He eyed her.

"You are lovely," she said.

Barnaby gave her the look of one who is well aware of his innate personal charms and placed a large foot on her boot.

"I could always take you for a quick walk," she mused.

At the word 'walk', Barnaby began leaping into the air, barking, panting and tugging at his lead.

Melissa laughed. "Hang on, hang on," she said, untying the lead. "I'll have to ask . . ."

Asking was not on the agenda. Barnaby, instantly transformed from placid, dopey mongrel to high-speed greyhound with attitude, bounded down Church Hill, zigzagging across the pavement and occasionally lifting all four feet off thc ground in a huge leap of joy.

Melissa, running after him in a desperate attempt to keep a hold on the lead, began laughing. He was so gloriously stupid.

Barnaby suddenly veered right down Spectacle Lane and galloped purposefully on.

Issy hadn't a clue where he was heading. And she didn't really care. For the first time since arriving in Mannings Green, she actually felt happy.

CHAPTER THREE
HOME THOUGHTS

WHILE BARNABY WAS TAKING Melissa on a mystery tour of Mannings Green, the Cortlesham to Victoria express was speeding her father towards the grey environs of London, and the delight he felt as the green fields of Sussex and Surrey gave way to the red roofs of suburbia, was certainly no less than his daughter's pleasure in being dragged down village lanes by a canine with a power complex.

Hugo Bailey leaned back in his first class seat, closed his eyes and contemplated the two days that stretched ahead of him. A brief pang of guilt washed over him as he acknowledged the fact that he could, quite easily, have crammed all that he had to do into one day, gone up in the morning and caught a late train home to Mannings Green and been there to help Fay get things straight at home. But this thought was rapidly followed by a Technicolor image of the awful house in Church Hill, with its oppressive dark wood and ghastly selection of wallpaper and he knew that he would use whatever excuses he could find to spend as much time as possible in his airy, spacious studio flat in Primrose Hill.

It's not as though I am being selfish, he assured himself as the train pulled into East Croydon station. Artistic people needed just the right atmosphere in which to work, and his makeshift study in the spare room of their new home was certainly not it. Faint odours of rotting dung wafted through the window from the farmyard along the lane and, apart from the middle of the morning, when the primary school children had their playtime, it was unnervingly quiet.

His partners said they envied him.

"You are so lucky," Roger Willis had commented the week before. "I'd love some peace to work in. This office is so noisy, you can't hear yourself think."

Perhaps, thought Hugo now, pulling a copy of *Architectural Digest* from his bag and flicking half-heartedly through its pages, that was the problem. Perhaps when he was in Mannings Green he had too much time to think – about what he had imagined life would be like when he hit fifty, about what he had achieved and where he was going from here. About, in fact, just what his role in life would be from now on.

It was all very well for Fay – she had the rest of her life sussed. She had got this idea into her head about going into the church, and just done it; and now everyone was saying how wonderful she was and how committed, and how proud he must be of her. And of course he was. Really. He was.

Wasn't he the one who kept telling Melissa that she must support her mother and stop going on about missing London? Did he complain when their evenings were interrupted by some parishioner turning up on the doorstep with some problem that meant his wife had to sit in the living-room being sympathetic while he sorted out the kids' tea? Or moan when they went to bed and all Fay wanted to do was make notes for the next Sunday's sermon or read the minutes of some boring parish council meeting? No, he didn't. He didn't even flinch – well, not outwardly anyway – when elderly women in plastic rainhats called him Mr Curate Dear. He was, he told himself as the train rattled past Clapham Junction, about as tolerant as a husband could get.

And he deserved a bit of a respite. After all, Fay couldn't have done any of this without him. He had really been rather marvellous about this new job, and she was lucky he could still hold down a well-paid position; curates earned precious little and if it hadn't been for his partnership in Willis, Bailey and Plimm, all these ideas of good works would have gone out of the window.

Not that business was exactly booming these days. There was enough work to keep them going, but it was boring, routine stuff, nothing like the heady days of the eighties when he had won the Pinkerton Award for Innovative Office Design with his glass and chrome hexagonal tower for Wellfoods Inc. Nowadays, he seemed to spend his time designing extensions for solicitors' offices or drawing up plans for yet another conversion of a disused factory into a set of *bijou* apartments. It paid his salary but it didn't give him a buzz.

But London did. The city always made him feel that he had come alive. As the train pulled slowly into Victoria station, he stood up, grabbed his bag and strode eagerly to the door. He jumped on to the platform and joined the throng of bodies surging towards the ticket barrier.

Tomorrow he would get those plans for St Olaf's Court finalised and have lunch with Roger and maybe pop over to the Royal Academy and catch that exhibition.

And, of course, this evening there was the dinner with the Internet café people. That would give him a buzz – the project was exciting and, best of all, he'd be with . . . Stop it. He straightened his shoulders and quickened his pace. He mustn't think like that. He could justify time away from home, he could even feel self-righteous about the amount of work he would get through, but thinking about the real reason for getting so excited about the coming dinner – that was unforgivable.

Although it was work, of a sort. And so worthwhile. Such a challenge.

Perhaps he could. On a purely professional basis, of course.

He'd wait and see. See what developed.

He stepped into Buckingham Palace Road and the unmistakable odour of heavily polluted air hit his nostrils and the cacophony of noise from the evening rush hour traffic assailed his ears. Right now, they both seemed a whole lot sweeter than country air and incessant birdsong.

They made him feel, in fact, as if he were coming home.

The place still didn't feel like home, thought Fay Bailey, as she dragged herself wearily upstairs to make peace with her younger son. It didn't help that the whole house was decorated like something out of a very cheap 1950s movie, or that she had been so busy for the past two weeks that she still hadn't hung all the curtains or bought lampshades to brighten up the hideous wooden wall lights. It wasn't like her; when they had moved into the Highgate house she had worked night and day stripping wallpaper and painting ceilings until the place looked just right. She wanted to make a start here but there had been so much to do and so many people to meet in the two weeks since they arrived that she had barely had time to go to the supermarket, let alone choose wallpaper and paint. She had suggested to Hugo that he might like to make a start on the sitting-room, but her husband was used to designing magnificent layouts and then finding someone else to do the hard graft. She rather feared he was cooking up plans to gut the whole place and start again. Which he couldn't. Because this time the house wasn't theirs.

Number five Church Hill belonged to the church and had housed several curates since it was built in the mid 1930s, none of whom, it would appear, had been interested in interior design. It had been built in the grounds of the vicarage – an imposing residence with a double-fronted façade and shuttered windows – and looked, Fay thought in amusement, like a poor relation that had been allowed to camp out in the grounds as long as it didn't make a nuisance of itself. Its one saving grace was the garden – a vast expanse of lawn and rockeries, with five gnarled apple-trees at the bottom and an ancient woodshed which Danny had already annexed as a camp for him and his friends.

Fay smiled to herself as she always did when she thought of her youngest child. Not, of course, that she had favourites; what mother did? But Danny, the totally unplanned infant who had arrived on Christmas Eve looking like a very small, angry troll, with a shock of red hair and the ability to scream louder and longer than any other baby in the maternity unit, had such a cheerful disregard for life's problems, such boundless energy and complete inability to bear a grudge, that you couldn't help but adore him.

She was about to knock on his door – she was a firm believer in parental politeness – when it flew open and the object of her adoration careered straight into her stomach. Danny might be eleven years and four months but he, like Melissa, had inherited what they called their mother's shortness genes. Issy moaned about it all the time but Danny couldn't care less, particularly since he had decided after his first riding lesson the previous weekend that he was going to become a jockey. One could only hope the horse had nerves of steel.

"Oh, Mum – hi, listen, I've got it sussed. Truly, really."

A small, very sticky hand slipped into hers. "Come and see."

Fay allowed herself to be dragged into what appeared to be a refuse collection point but was in fact Danny's bedroom.

"There!" He pointed triumphantly at the table standing by the window.

In the middle stood a bright blue, upturned milk crate, its top and sides covered with aluminium foil. Inside were several sheets of newspaper, one of Fay's rather better saucers and a whole bag of cotton wool balls. Adorning the whole thing was a large sign written in blue and red felt tip which read:

"See, Mum," he said eagerly, beaming up at her. "He'd be quite safe and you wouldn't even have to see him, not ever."

Fay sighed. "Oh Danny, I don't know . . ." she began.

"He's frightfully educational," her son persisted earnestly, "and animals are relaxing – I'll probably be a much more together child."

Fay burst out laughing. "Oh all right!" she said. "But only if we buy a proper cage and . . ."

Two skinny arms flung themselves round her waist. "Thanks, Mum, you're a star!" he said. "Can I go and tell Sam now? Can I? He could bring Humphrey over and . . ."

"No way!" said his mother sternly. "Not until we've bought a cage and we can't do that until Saturday. You will just have to be patient. You can phone him."

"OK," said Danny cheerfully, content to mollify his mother now that he had his own way. "You know, we could get Humphrey a wife and then they'd have babies and that'd be education . . ."

He caught sight of his mother's expression and thought better of it. "Just joking," he said. "Wait till I tell Issy – she'll go mega manic."

I can well believe it, thought Fay with a sigh, watching her son career down the stairs. These days, Melissa could go manic over the appearance of one small spot, never mind the addition of a large rat to the family unit. And of course, every problem that beset her was her mother's fault; not only had the spots apparently appeared because she was fed the wrong breakfast cereal as a child, but she was now totally without any hope of a social life because of her mother's indiscretion in her choice of job. I'm probably responsible for global warming as well, Fay thought wryly, eyeing the debris on Danny's floor and half-heartedly picking up a pile of football cards.

"Now don't you be worrying yourself with all that, Reverend dear!"

Connie appeared in the doorway, plastic mac over her arm and rainhat firmly in place, despite the shafts of sunlight flooding the bedroom. "I'll do that when I come on Friday. Tell her it's on the bed."

Fay blinked. Connie's ability to change subject mid-sentence was a little confusing. "Pardon?"

"Melissa's skirt, dear. She fell over and tore the hem. No problem, I've mended it."

"Oh Connie, you are a treasure! I hope she said thank you."

Connie beamed. "I'm sure she would have done if she'd been here. But she's not. He's gone too. But then, they're young, the both of them."

"Gone? If Daniel's run off . . ."

"No dear, not the little lad. Melissa and Barnaby."

She marched to the window and gestured at the unoccupied lamppost.

"You mean, she's not in her room doing her homework?"

Connie shook her head. "Not to worry," she said. "Between you and me, I reckon you can have too much of book learning."

"Not," said Fay firmly, "in Melissa's case."

"Oh well," said Connie equably, "no harm done. She can bring him round to my place when she gets back – number four Mill Lane, the one with the purple door. Not that I'm partial to purple myself, but my Albert chose it the week before he died and I don't like to change . . ."

"Quite, quite," said Fay soothingly, wondering whether Connie actually talked non-stop in her sleep.

"So you'll ask her to pop him round when she gets back?"

"I think," said Fay grimly, "I might be too busy wringing her neck."

CHAPTER FOUR
BRIEF ENCOUNTER

"COME ON, BARNABY – IF WE don't get a move on, Mum'll murder me. Home!"

The big dog stopped in the middle of his nose-tip investigation of an empty milk carton in the gutter outside HappyMart, and looked at Melissa with the withering expression of one who has no time for such ridiculous suggestions.

She yanked the lead. Barnaby planted his four huge feet firmly in the centre of the pavement and yawned.

Melissa tugged.

Barnaby lay down.

"It might have been better to get a dachshund!" A voice from behind caused Melissa to jump.

She turned round to see the most devastatingly fit boy sitting on the stone wall of the neighbouring cottage. He had wavy, caramel-coloured hair flopping over one eye and huge milk chocolate eyes. Propped beside him was a bright orange skateboard.

He was to die for.

He grinned at her and a small dimple appeared in his chin.

Melissa opened her mouth and shut it again. It appeared that the power of speech had suddenly deserted her.

"Little people need little dogs!" chuckled the guy, jumping off the wall and ostentatiously flicking the skateboard on to its wheels with his foot.

As he stood up, Melissa realised that he was not only a total dish but that he was tall. Very tall. In fact, she found that the top of her head was about on a level with his ribs, a fact which simply served to emphasise his snide remark about her lack of inches. Standing beside him, she felt like some dippy kid.

He grabbed Barnaby's lead from her hand. "Get up, you silly mongrel!"

Barnaby knew defeat when he saw it and meekly stood up as though butter wouldn't melt in his mouth.

"I could have managed!" Melissa snatched the lead away from him, furious at being made to look an idiot. "I wasn't really trying."

She glared at Barnaby who had the good grace to look away.

"Sure you weren't," said the guy, unwrapping a sliver of chewing-gum and putting it into his mouth. "You need to shorten his lead and make him walk to heel. Let him know who's boss."

"Thanks very much, but I don't need your advice," snapped Melissa.

"Oooh – fiery with it, must be the red hair!" grinned

the guy, jumping on to the skateboard and balancing on one leg. "I'm Matt, by the way. Matt Carter. You must be new around here – I guess I'd have spotted you and this hound if you'd been here long!"

Melissa tried to look cool and disinterested. "We moved in a couple of weeks ago," she said. "I'm Melissa. And Barnaby's not mine – I'm walking him for a friend."

"I would have said," drawled Matt, "that it was debatable exactly who is walking who!"

"Oh very funny!" retorted Melissa and stomped off down the road towards Church Hill. Pompous git. Making her look like a total dweeb. What business had he to patronise her like that?

Not that she cared. After all, she didn't even know the guy. Probably wouldn't ever see him again. And if she did, he'd probably ignore her. Not that it mattered to her one way or the other.

As she reached the corner, Matt skateboarded past her on the opposite side of the road, executing a very showy jump turn. Out of the corner of her eye, she saw him wave as he flipped the skateboard round into the High Street and noted that he had the cutest bum, but she made a point of ignoring him, firmly pulling on Barnaby's lead and talking to him in what she hoped were authoritative terms.

But as soon as she rounded the corner, she realised that it might have been more advisable to stay outside the shop and be insulted by a stranger.

Her mother was standing at the gate of their house,

looking up and down the road and clenching and unclenching her fists in the manner of a parent who has had about as much as they can take. Bustling down the pavement towards Melissa was Connie, plastic mac flapping in the breeze.

"There you are, well, I said you'd be fine but she's got a lot on her plate and mothers do worry, don't they, so I'll be taking him and you go and look busy with them books."

Connie took Barnaby's lead. "Come on, you, come with Connie."

Barnaby threw Melissa a pleading look and hesitated. But the sight of Fay Bailey striding purposefully down the road towards him was obviously more alarming than the thought of leaving his new playmate and, giving her left hand a quick slobber, he turned, heaved a deep sigh and padded reluctantly after Connie.

"And just where do you think you have been, young lady?" demanded her mother, whose neck above the tight edge of her dog-collar was decidedly pink.

"Sorry," said Melissa meekly. "I took Barnaby for a walk and . . ."

"Oh, you did, did you?" retorted her mother. "And you didn't think to let me know?"

"Well, I was going to but . . ."

"Just don't start making excuses!" interjected her mother, turning back towards the house. "I specifically told you to come in and do your homework and you deliberately defied me."

"Oh come on, Mum, chill out!" Melissa protested. "It's no big deal."

"Frankly, Melissa, it is a very big deal indeed!" replied her mother, her voice rising. "What you have to realise is . . ."

But what it was she was supposed to realise Melissa didn't hear. To her horror, coming down the road behind her mother's bristling back, arms linked, were Tara and Ellie. And they were looking straight at her. And tittering.

". . . and besides, I hadn't a clue where you were and anything might have happened . . ."

"Mum! Shut up!" hissed Melissa, fixing a sort of sick smile on her face and hoping that her friends would think she and her mum were having an amiable bicker.

"Don't you speak to me like that! And stop smirking!"

Any hopes of deluding Ellie and Tara went out of the window as her mother's voice rose to an unholy crescendo.

"Hi, Melissa!" Tara said coyly as they ambled past.

"Hi, Mrs – Reverend Bailey," simpered Ellie and spluttered into giggles.

"Hello," said Melissa weakly.

Her mother stopped in mid-flow and replaced her furious frown with a sweet smile. "Evening, girls," she began. "Now let me see . . ."

But Ellie and Tara had quickened their step and were already turning the corner into Spectacle Lane.

"Friends of yours?" queried her mother, opening the gate.

"Friends? Thanks to you, I probably won't have any friends ever again!" Melissa slammed the gate and stomped up the path and through the open front door.

"Me? What have I done?" asked her mother, following behind.

"Oh nothing, nothing at all!" retorted Melissa sarcastically, marching down the hall and into the kitchen. "You just don't get it, do you? I spend the whole week trying to tell people that you're just a normal mother, and that you're not all holier-than-thou and stuff – and then what do you do? Go and humiliate me in front of my friends – and all because I went for a walk!"

Her mother bit her lip and counted to ten. "I didn't know they were there – and besides, you don't understand – you can't just go swanning off with a strange dog and not expect me to worry."

"I thought," said Melissa, "that you said the country would be so much safer than London."

Got you, she thought.

"That dog might have been really dangerous," riposted her mother. "You can't be too careful."

"Him? Dangerous? He's just soppy."

She gave her mum a half-smile. An idea was forming in her head and she knew from experience that her mother softened rapidly when Issy switched on the charm.

"He is cute, though," she said more calmly. "And he's so funny. Shall I lay the table?"

She knew that before mentioning her idea she should transform herself into helpful offspring mode.

"Thanks." Her mother looked somewhat surprised but highly relieved that the current drama appeared to be over. "And go and call the boys, will you?"

"I was thinking," said Melissa tentatively, after she had not only called her brothers, but laid the table, tidied the counter top, emptied the pedal bin and even wiped out the microwave, "it must be hard for Connie getting lumbered with a dog at her age."

"Mmm," said her mother, quite obviously not anticipating her daughter's next move.

"Can I have him?" Melissa blurted out, as her mother lifted a casserole from the oven.

Fay looked at her as if she had suggested opening a small zoo in the back garden. "Have Barnaby? You mean, here?"

No, on Mars, thought Melissa, but said nothing. "Please?"

"Of course you can't, don't be so ridiculous. Do you think I've got time to be running around after smelly dogs?"

"He's not smelly!" shouted Melissa, "and anyway, you've got time to run around after half the parish. You've got time to be all holy and sweet as sugar to everyone else. If it wasn't for you I wouldn't need a dog!"

Her mother closed her eyes and sighed.

"What dog? Are we getting a dog?" Danny burst through the kitchen door, a blob of orange felt-tip pen on his nose.

"There's a dog breeding Web site on the Internet." Ben ambled behind, his nose in *Net News*. "Shall I check it out?"

"We are not – repeat not – getting a dog," said their mother firmly, draining vegetables over the kitchen sink.

"That's good, 'cos I don't think Humphrey would like it much," commented Danny, pulling out his chair and sitting down.

Melissa's eyes widened. "You're not – Mum, you haven't said he can have that rat?"

Her mother coloured slightly and paid great attention to mashing potatoes.

"Yup," said Danny. "He's going to have a cage and live in my room and . . ."

"That is SO unfair!" Issy exploded. "He can have some evil little rodent but you won't let me have Barnaby."

"That's completely different," said her mother, dumping a plate of chicken casserole in front of her.

"Oh, well it would be, wouldn't it?" expostulated Melissa. "We all know that what Danny wants, Danny gets, don't we? Why can't . . ."

Her mother went to the fridge and poured herself a glass of white wine, which she downed with alarming haste. "Melissa, not now. Please. I want to eat my supper in peace. Say grace, will you, please."

Melissa closed her eyes. "For what we are about to receive may the Lord make us truly thankful Amen. I would look after him myself, Mum, honestly and . . ."

"We'll talk about it later," said her mother, opting for the age-old parental cop-out. "I've got a Youth Liaison Committee meeting at eight and it looks so bad if I'm late for . . ."

"Oh great!" Melissa whirled round to face her. "So it's OK for you to liaise with everyone else's kids, but you can't spare the time to listen to your own!"

"Issy," said Ben.

"Yes?"

"Do me a favour?"

"What?"

"Shut up."

He hadn't meant to snap at his sister. It was just that he couldn't be doing with all this childish chitchat, not when he had so much on his mind. In some ways, he envied Melissa and Danny. All they had to think about was dogs and rats and whether they could get out of helping with the washing-up. Life hadn't suddenly got complicated for them like it had for him.

"No pudding for me," he said, pushing back his chair and standing up.

His mother looked up, concern written all over her face. "Darling, you've only picked at your chicken; are you all right?"

"Fine," said Ben, edging towards the door. "Just lots of work to get through, that's all."

"He just wants to go and be boring in front of a computer as per usual," commented Melissa, who was feeling miffed with the entire universe and found her brother an easy outlet for her frustrations. "Are you ever going to get a life, Ben?"

"Oh shut up, can't you? Just shut up!"

"Ben!" His mother's eyes widened in horror. "What's got into you?"

Ben said nothing but merely slammed the kitchen door and went upstairs. How could he answer her? He didn't know what had got into him. That was the problem.

And worse still, there was no one he could talk to about it. No one at all.

CHAPTER FIVE
WHAT THE EYE DOESN'T SEE . . .

WHILE HIS CHILDREN WERE getting up one another's noses in Mannings Green, Hugo Bailey was propping up the bar at *Le Petit Poisson*, waiting for his clients and thinking how delightful it was to have a whole evening when his peace would not be disrupted by a churchwarden with a fit of pique or a couple of dewy-eyed youngsters arriving for marriage preparation classes. As if, he thought wryly, anything prepared you for that.

He took a long gulp of gin and tonic and felt immediately more mellow. Really, it wouldn't be so bad. If he could manage just two nights a week up here, he could play the role of supportive and understanding spouse for the rest of the time. And of course there would be the odd occasion when the wrong sort of leaf fell on the main Victoria to Cortlesham line, or the drivers on the London Underground went on strike and then he might have to stretch it to three nights or even a whole week.

His hopeful contemplation of future transport disruption was interrupted by the arrival of Theo Hirst, his latest client, a lean and angular man with iron-grey hair and the sort of rugged features that made women simper and spill their white wine spritzers. And with him, looking elegant and alluring in dove grey, was the firm's newest trainee, Joanna Lockley.

Hugo's heartbeat quickened. His eyes travelled from her silky blonde hair, down the length of her trim frame to her slender ankles. He shook himself. He was not here to ogle Joanna. He was here to convince Theo Hirst that two million pounds was a fair price for his new Internet café. But of course, Joanna had been assigned to him, to learn more about the business, more about negotiating skills. And it was only right that he should show an interest in a young woman with such obvious talent.

"Theo!" Hugo held out a hand and smiled warmly. "And Joanna, my dear. How very, very good to see you – both."

"We did it!" Hugo thumped the table in triumph and gestured to a passing waiter. "He's on board!"

Joanna smiled at him and sipped her coffee. "It was all because of you," she said. "You were brilliant. I do so admire your work."

Hugo smiled. "Soon to be overshadowed by this new project of yours, I don't doubt."

Joanna dropped her eyes. "I don't suppose – well, could I run a few ideas past you? I'm not sure I am making the best use of the space available."

"Of course," said Hugo. "I'm fascinated by your designs, they have such flair and . . ."

He hesitated. This was ridiculous. He sounded like some star-struck teenager drooling over a pop star, not a fifty-one-year-old architect in conversation with a trainee half his age. Besides, it was late. He should be getting home. Home! He hadn't phoned Fay.

He glanced at his watch. Ten thirty. He'd just have one more brandy and then call her from the restaurant payphone.

Joanna reached out and touched his hand. A shiver went through him.

"Are you sure you don't mind? I mean, staying on a bit while I show you my sketches?"

Hugo smiled. "Mind? I can't think of anything I'd rather do."

Melissa hung her clothes on the back of the bedroom door and padded along the landing in her pyjamas to the bathroom. If she was going for the mature and sophisticated look, she might as well do it properly. No way was she giving Ellie and Tara the chance to laugh at her ever again.

She locked the door, grabbed the tweezers and began plucking furiously at her eyebrows. After ten minutes, during which she had sneezed fifty-four times and used half a box of tissues mopping up her streaming eyes, she was left with two razor-thin lines of palest ginger brow and a very red patch over her nose. She dragged her hair tightly back off her face and surveyed the effect critically. She definitely looked older. All she had to do now was varnish her nails with that amazing new Glitter'n'Glo polish and the look would be complete. Of course, coloured varnish wasn't allowed at Furze Grange, but then she could always say she was new and didn't know the rules. By the time they'd made her take it off her mates would have sussed that she was totally cool and up for it. They would be well impressed.

It was only as she was climbing into bed that she found herself wondering whether Matt Carter would see her, and if he would be equally amazed by the transformation in her appearance. Not that what he thought mattered in the slightest. But still.

Fay picked up the bedside telephone and dialled Hugo's number.

"I am sorry, but I am not available to take your call . . ." The answerphone cut in, Hugo's voice sounding impersonal and stilted.

"Damn!" she hissed beneath her breath and then looked heavenwards. "Sorry."

Where was he? He had promised to phone when he got to the flat; she had checked with the kids and he hadn't called while she was out.

They always talked every night when he was away. When they lived in London and he had gone all over Europe to conferences, she had never gone to sleep without saying goodnight over the phone. It felt all wrong.

She wanted to tell him all about the meeting and how the committee thought her plan was stunning. And she had to remind him to go to John Lewis and pick up the fabric for the new sitting-room curtains – and maybe he could find a pet shop and get a cage for Danny's rat. No, come to think of it, best not say anything about Humphrey until Hugo got home.

She whispered a sloppy message on to the answerphone and settled down to sleep.

At the corner table in *Le Petit Poisson*, lingering over his third large espresso, her husband gazed into

Joanna Lockley's huge grey eyes and told her for the fifth time that evening how very much he admired her work.

CHAPTER SIX
CANINES AND HAUTE COUTURE

THERE HAD BEEN, THOUGHT MELISSA the following morning, one major flaw in her plan to look seriously sassy. Her mother. If Issy had appeared at breakfast in anything other than strict regulation uniform, her mum would have been sure to read the riot act and send her straight back upstairs to transform herself into Miss Goody Two-shoes.

Which was why she was now sitting at the table with the morning paper spread over her knees in an attempt to hide the hemline of her skirt and a sweater covering up her shirt and vest top, shovelling bran flakes down her throat and pretending to be hugely interested in an article about the Millennium Dome.

In the event her mother was too busy making sandwiches and preventing Danny from practising trotting on the back of one of the kitchen chairs to notice what her daughter was doing.

"Danny, for the last time, will you stop doing that?"

"But I've got riding on Saturday and we're doing rising trots," he began.

"Not on my furniture, you're not – now just go upstairs and get your stuff ready for school!"

"OK," said Danny equably, jumping off the chair. "I need chocolate."

"You are not having sweets at this time of day," asserted his mother.

"Not to eat, silly, for cookery," remonstrated Danny. "We're doing chocolate fudge brownies. We each take something different. I'm chocolate."

His mother sighed. "You might have told me," she said. "You'll just have to run down to HappyMart and get some."

She thrust a couple of one-pound coins into her son's hand. "Now get a move on and come straight back!"

Danny nodded and hurtled to the front door.

Seconds later, there was a squeal, a yelp and the sound of child hitting stone.

"Good heavens! Now what's he done?" Mrs Bailey dashed up the hallway.

"I don't believe it!" Her mother's exclamation was followed by an outburst of excited barking.

Melissa forgot all about camouflage, dropped the newspaper on the floor and sped to the door. Her brother was sprawled on the front step, and standing with his two front feet firmly on his chest, affectionately licking his neck, was Barnaby.

"Barnaby!" Melissa cried. "You came back!"

At the sound of her voice, Barnaby abruptly ceased his ministrations on Danny and bounded over to her, thrusting a damp nose against her knee-length boot and panting with ecstasy.

"See, he really wants to be here," Issy exclaimed, grabbing his collar. "Oh Mum, please let's keep him. He needs looking after."

"He needs locking up," muttered her mother. "Danny darling, are you all right? What happened?"

"He was on the doorstep. I fell over him. I could . . ." he paused for effect, ". . . have been killed."

"No such luck," muttered Melissa.

Across the road, the clock on the tower of St Peter's struck eight.

"I've got to go," said their mother. "Morning prayers. Melissa, you'll have to take this wretched animal back to Connie's and . . ."

She paused and eyed her daughter. "Just what," she said in the measured tones of a parent who has just realised that all is not as it should be, "have you got on?"

Melissa's brain went into overdrive. "Gracious, is that the time? I'll miss the bus."

She thrust Barnaby at her mother, grabbed her blazer from the coat hook, slung her schoolbag over her shoulder and pushed past her brother and down the path.

"Melissa, just come back here this instant and . . ."

"Bye, Mum, have a good day. Bye, Barnaby!"

At the sound of his name, Barnaby leaped into the air and executed a ninety degree turn, landing on Mrs Bailey's left foot. At the same instant, the telephone in the hall began shrilling urgently and the vicar appeared in the church porch opposite, beckoning furiously to his curate and pointing to his watch.

As she sped along the pavement, Melissa heard her mother ordering Danny inside and, with a quick glance over her shoulder, noted with satisfaction that Barnaby was following them with the air of one who intends to make himself wholly at home.

"Thank you, God," whispered Melissa. "I owe you one."

Hugo drummed his fingers on the table and waited for someone to pick up the phone. He should have phoned the night before, but it had been nearly midnight by the time he had got home.

"Danny? Is that you? It's Dad."

He paused, his ears assaulted by a stream of garbled conversation which had something to do with dogs and rats and Issy being for it.

"Is Mum there?" he said when his son finally stopped to draw breath. "Fay? Darling, so sorry I didn't call you last night. Deadly dinner – just went on and on."

An image of just what went on flashed into his mind and he promptly pushed the disturbing memory away.

"What? Bad moment? Oh right. Morning prayers.

John Lewis? No, no, of course I won't forget. OK, darling, I'll let you go. Call you tonight. Love you lots."

He replaced the receiver and stood staring into space. At least the last bit wasn't a lie. He did love her. Lots.

So why was it that as he piled papers into his briefcase in readiness for his morning meeting, the only face that kept swimming before his eyes belonged to the beautiful, enchanting, fascinating Joanna Lockley?

Melissa stopped a few metres short of the bus stop, where a clutch of noisy year sevens and eights were being infantile with a football, and leaned against the wall. She pulled off her sweater, ramming it into her schoolbag, and unfastened the top two buttons of her shirt. Ferreting in the pocket of the blazer she had no intention of wearing, she took out her folding mirror and applied three layers of Pink Chocolate lipstick. To the discreet gold studs already in her ears she added a star, a fish and a large silver question-mark and then, ramming her mega cool, white beanie hat on her head, she sauntered up to the bus stop.

Just then, a guy on a mountain bike cycled past and glanced in her direction. Seconds later he did a double-take, wobbled and stopped.

"Hey it's you! Hi!"

Matt Carter gave her an appraising glance, his eyes travelling from the top of her head to her feet and back up again, stopping at around thigh level.

"I didn't recognise you," he said.

Oh goodie, thought Melissa.

"Love the hat!" he said admiringly. "Say – who won? You or the dog?"

Melissa's failure to think of a witty riposte was saved by the approach of the Furze Grange school bus. Any stirrings of annoyance at his flippant manner were firmly quashed when she caught sight of Ellie and Tara, sitting in the front seat of the top deck, staring out of the window. Straight at them.

"See you around," she called loudly to Matt in the hope that her mates would hear and with that she jumped on to the bus and clattered up the stairs, pretending to be totally disdainful of the couple of whistles and "Wh-oah!"s from the guys on the bottom deck.

"Hi!" she said casually to the girls, sinking down in the nearest vacant seat and pulling a textbook from her bag. "How's things?"

Ellie and Tara were staring at her open-mouthed.

"That is such a cool hat," breathed Tara.

"Never mind the hat," interrupted Ellie. "Was that Matt Carter I saw you talking to?"

"What?" Melissa tried to look detached. "Oh yes, yes it was."

"You said you didn't have a boyfriend," Ellie said accusingly.

"I didn't say I didn't have loads of friends who were boys," Melissa replied.

"And Matt's one of them?"

"Oh yeah," said Melissa coolly, crossing her fingers under her book.

Ellie looked at her with new respect.

"You look really cool," said Tara. "Although Mrs Fisher will have you strung up when she sees you."

Melissa shrugged, as if facing the dubious justice of her year tutor was of no importance to her whatsoever.

"Does your mum know?" Ellie asked. "I mean, she seemed pretty wound up last night. I would have thought she'd be the sort of person to go ape and . . ."

"My personal image is not up to my mother," said Melissa loftily. "I am my own person."

"Shove up, Tara," Ellie ordered. "Let Issy come and sit with us."

I'm in! thought Melissa joyfully. I really think that at last I am in.

"Appear in school once more looking like that and you will be in detention!" Mrs Fisher pursed her thin lips and looked at Issy as if she had recently crawled out of a particularly unsavoury sewer. "I can not imagine what possessed you."

Melissa looked at her in wide-eyed innocence, fully aware that the attention of most of the year ten tutor group B was on her. "But, miss, what have I done wrong?"

"You mean aside from the ironmongery in your ears and those very loud tights? You are not wearing a regulation shirt, and you have that – that garment underneath and . . ."

"It's a vest top, miss," volunteered Tara helpfully. "Everyone's wearing them."

"Not in this school, they are not!" asserted the teacher. "I am prepared to ignore the shortness of your skirt, since half the pupils here seem to be wearing pelmets . . ."

"Old joke, yawn, yawn," whispered Ellie into Melissa's left ear.

". . . but tackiness of dress I will not tolerate. This is a place of learning, not a Paris catwalk. You have five minutes to go to the cloakrooms and render yourself in a fit state to attend class."

Melissa smiled her sweetest smile. "Yes, Mrs Fisher," she said, quite content to obey now that her friends knew she was spunky.

"I am quite sure," added the teacher, "that your mother would be appalled if she saw you. It is quite an affront to her calling."

Oh no you don't, thought Melissa. Don't you drag that up again and undo all the good I've done.

"My mother says that God made us all unique and it is up to us to explore our individuality," she replied.

For a moment, Mrs Fisher looked fazed. "Yes, well, doubtless – oh, just go and tidy yourself up!"

As Issy crossed to the classroom door, Tara winked at her and Ellie gave her the thumbs-up sign. Even Flick Thomas, who spent his whole life putting down the girls, whispered, "Good on you, titch," as she closed the door behind her.

She bounded down the stairs to the girls' locker room with a spring in her step. It was turning out to be a very good day.

CHAPTER SEVEN
CHANCE MEETINGS

THE NEW CURATE OF ST PETER'S was having a rather less auspicious morning. Not only had she arrived late, out of breath and covered in dog hairs for morning prayers, but on the way home, while she was still trying to calm down over the antics of her daughter, Mrs Cumberforth-Jones, a woman of large hips and an even larger opinion of herself, had accosted her outside the church.

"Ah, Fay, my dear," she had begun. Mrs Cumberforth-Jones liked to consider herself on intimate terms with the clergy of all ranks, presumably because she believed her place in paradise would be assured if she could say that she had entertained bishops and deacons alike to chilled chardonnay and canapés at Glebe House. "And how are you settling in?"

"Very well, thank you," Fay had replied. If you omit white rats, rampant dogs, forgetful husbands and daughters with attitude.

"Now I don't want you to think that I am interfering," intoned Mrs C-J, who was obviously planning to do just that, "only I couldn't help noticing your daughter."

Few people can, thought Fay. Melissa is not one to blend in with the background.

"And I do feel, dear, that as God's representative in the village you do need to maintain certain standards."

Fay bit her lip.

"And the child's attire – well, if you don't mind my saying so, it was rather – unsuitable."

"For what, Mrs Cumberforth-Jones? For potholing? Sky-diving?"

The simpering smile on her parishioner's lips faded. "For anything. I am no prude but that skirt was . . ."

"Too short. I do agree. I shall be dealing with it."

The smile returned. "I knew you'd see it my way, dear. As the daughter of God's representative she needs to be setting an example and . . ."

"Mrs Cumberforth-Jones . . ."

"Call me Lavinia, dear."

Fay said a quick prayer for calm. Obviously the lines to heaven were engaged. "Lavinia, I rather think that God, should he have nothing better to do this morning than assess Melissa's suitability as a curate's daughter – which considering the state of the world I doubt – would be looking at something more important than the height of her hemline – her love of life and sense of humour, for instance."

"Well, yes, of course, but this parish is full of

wayward young people . . ."

"This parish, Mrs Cumberforth-Jones, is full of young people searching for answers. I do have a few ideas on how to go about helping them find these answers, but believe me, fretting about what they wear is not one of them. Now if you will excuse me . . ."

Lavinia sniffed, swallowed and turned to leave. "I'm sure you know what you're doing, reverend," she acknowledged in tones which suggested she wasn't sure at all. "I shall watch with interest to see what you have in mind."

I bet you will, Fay had thought, trudging home. It would be quite nice if I knew. It was easy to stand up at a committee meeting as she had the evening before, and hold forth about making the church more accessible to the young, and dispelling the image of a stuffy, self-satisfied clique of pious do-gooders (that had got the churchwardens going) but actually coming up with the goods might not prove so easy.

She let herself into the house and walked through to the kitchen, gingerly opening the door as if not quite certain what horrors awaited her. Lying in the middle of the floor, paws crossed angelically, and wearing a 'Haven't I been the most amazingly good dog?' expression was Barnaby, in exactly the same place where she had left him an hour earlier.

At the sight of his reluctant benefactress, he began thumping his tail enthusiastically on the quarry-tiled floor and wriggling in joy.

Fay bent down and ruffled his coat. "Issy's right, you know," she admitted. "You are rather cute."

Barnaby's tail went into overdrive.

"And you're obviously too much for Connie to control," she went on.

Barnaby, sensing victory, rolled over and stuck all four feet in the air.

"And if I let you stay, I would earn brownie points with Issy."

Which could be very useful. Because if she was going to put her plans into action, she needed Issy's help. And right now, the chances of getting that were about as high as of snow falling in the Arizona desert.

It was said that God moved in mysterious ways. Barnaby could just, after all, be the answer to her prayers.

She picked up the phone and dialled Connie's number.

It was while Melissa was scrubbing the last traces of lipstick from her mouth that she spotted the girl. She was coming out of one of the toilet cubicles and it was quite clear, even from a distance, that she had been crying. Her eye caught Issy's and she immediately looked away and hurried over to a washbasin in the far corner of the room.

Issy finished what she was doing and dried her hands on a paper towel. She paused and looked over to the girl. She was standing at the basin splashing water on her face and her shoulders were shaking silently.

Melissa fished in her pocket and pulled out a handkerchief. "It's not awfully clean, I'm afraid, but it's all I've got."

"Thanks." The girl grabbed it but didn't look at Melissa.

Issy hesitated. "You're in my year, aren't you? In Mrs MacDonald's class?"

The girl nodded and this time she looked up at Melissa. Her eyes were red, as if she had been crying for a long time, and her light brown, wavy hair was tousled as if she had spent the last hour running her fingers through it.

"Isn't she the mega strict one?" Issy asked conversationally, as the girl blew her nose and wiped her eyes.

The faintest smile crossed her lips. "Tell me about it," she said. "She'll go ape at me when I go back."

She paused and eyed Melissa. "Aren't you the girl whose mum's a priest? Sorry, I don't know your name."

Here we go, thought Issy. "Melissa. Yes, she's the curate at Mannings Green."

"Oh, right. I'm Kirsty – Kirsty Hunt. Here," and she thrust the soggy handkerchief back at Melissa.

"Keep it," said Issy. "You can give it back any old time."

In the distance the bell rang.

"Look, I'd better go," she said. "I'm in enough trouble as it is – for daring to wear something halfway decent!" She grinned. Kirsty gave her a watery smile.

"Are you going to be OK?"

Kirsty nodded. "And Melissa?"

"Yes?"

"Thanks."

Melissa looked at her in surprise. "What for?"

"For not making fun of me – and for not asking loads of questions."

Melissa smiled and shrugged. "I guess if you want to tell me stuff, you will. You can, you know. I'm not going any place. Regrettably."

This time Kirsty smiled a proper smile, a smile which made her azure eyes dance and made Melissa realise just how pretty she was. "I'll catch you later maybe? I mean, not if . . ."

"Great," said Melissa. "That would be great. And thank you, too."

Kirsty looked puzzled.

"For not making some crack about holy mothers and things."

"Why would I?"

"People do."

CHAPTER EIGHT
FRIENDSHIPS CEMENTED

"STILL RECOVERING FROM LAST NIGHT?"

Joanna leaned over Hugo's left shoulder and grinned as he stifled a yawn. A strand of her shoulder-length blonde hair rested on his collar.

"Oh – no, I'm fine. Good evening, lots of progress made." He glanced nervously round the open-plan office, anxious that none of his colleagues should spot them together and start any silly rumours.

She pulled back, aware that he was being very cool with her.

"I think your ideas are terrific," he said hastily. "I really do admire what you are trying to do."

Her face broke into an eager smile. "Thanks," she said huskily. "Although it's one thing to have the ideas and quite another to put them into practice. That's where your advice is so invaluable. You're so exciting to talk to."

Hugo preened inwardly. It was a long time since anyone had found him exciting, particularly someone as vibrant and beautiful as Joanna.

"Anyway," she continued briskly, "I sat up half the night making the changes you suggested and I think I may have got it right. I don't suppose – no, no that's being selfish."

"What?"

"Well, I thought – maybe we could meet and look

through them some time?"

Hugo thought fast. This was not a good idea. Joanna was half his age, single and enticingly beautiful. He knew that if he agreed to her suggestion, it would be for all the wrong reasons.

He would say no. Tell her to talk to Roger or Dickon or one of the other partners. It was the only sensible thing to do.

"Hugo?" Two fingers brushed across his hand. "Could you bear to?"

Don't do it, Hugo told himself.

"Of course, Jo," he beamed. "Nothing would give me greater pleasure."

Ben Bailey stood outside the computer room at Cortlesham College, nervously fiddling with his polo neck. She was in there already. Perhaps if he waited for a bit till all the seats near by were taken, he could sidle in unnoticed.

"No good standing there drooling, Ben – get in there, mate!"

He turned to find Matt Carter eyeing him teasingly.

Ben tried to look nonchalant. "I've just remembered I left some software in my locker," he improvised. "I'll catch you in a minute."

Matt raised his eyebrows. "You're out of it, man," he said. "You've got a girl like Vicki giving you the come-on and you chicken out! You wouldn't find me hanging back. What's wrong with you?"

That's the problem, thought Ben miserably as he

hurried up the corridor. I don't *know* what's wrong with me. Every other guy my age knows how to talk to girls. And do a lot more besides. And here I am, seventeen and two months and I've never even kissed a girl properly. Even Mum's beginning to make pointed remarks.

He reached the lockers, turned round and began heading back to the computer room. As he opened the door, a sea of faces turned to look at him, most of them grinning broadly from ear to ear.

The only seat left in the whole room was next to Vicki Landcross. Who had crossed her legs and was looking at him provocatively from beneath her long black eyelashes.

"In your own time, Mr Bailey," commented the lecturer sarcastically.

Ben felt his face flood with colour. There was nothing for it. He'd have to sit next to her.

He just hoped the whole room couldn't hear his heart beating.

"You were so cool with old Fishface earlier," said Ellie as she and Melissa lined up to collect a plate of what the school menu sheet said was pasta bake.

"When you said that about your mum and God, she was utterly and totally gobsmacked!" giggled Tara. "Was it true?"

Melissa grinned. "Oh, she did say it, once. In a sermon. I don't somehow think she was referring to school uniform though."

"I wish I could get a top like the one you were wearing," sighed Ellie. "Where did you find it?"

"Glad Rags. In the sale."

Her friends stared at her blankly.

"It's this wicked clothes shop in London," Melissa said. "I used to get loads of gear there – it's really off-the-wall stuff."

"Great," sighed Ellie, gesturing to three empty spaces at a corner table. "That's the end of that idea, then. I wanted something really cool to wear to my party . . ."

Tara nudged her and pulled a face.

"What? Oh it's OK. I'm inviting Issy."

Melissa tried not to look too pleased.

"You said . . ." began Tara.

"Shut up," said Ellie, stuffing pasta into her mouth. "I changed my mind, OK?" She turned to Mellisa. "It's two weeks on Saturday – if I can find anything worth wearing, that is. Which is unlikely in Cortlesham."

"So go to London," said Melissa, who had never considered shopping anywhere else.

"Oh yeah, just like that!" said Ellie. "Besides, I wouldn't know where to start. It's so huge and those Underground maps are unreal."

Melissa burst out laughing and then stopped. After all, she had lived there all her life. It must seem a bit daunting after Cortlesham.

"I know," she said, pulling the ring off a can of lemonade, "why don't we all go? I know where all the trendy shops are – and we could hit the markets too, get some great jewellery and hats and stuff."

Her friends' eyes widened in delight.

"We could too," enthused Ellie. "That would be brill. Not this Saturday, though. I'll need at least a week to talk my mum into parting with the cash."

"So how about next Saturday?" suggested Melissa, already excited at the thought of getting back to London.

"You're on!"

They all slapped hands.

"You know," said Ellie, scraping her plate as if food was going out of fashion, "you're not drippy after all."

"Thanks," said Melissa with a wry grin. "Thanks a bundle."

Ellie and Tara were staying late for basketball practice, so Melissa caught the Mannings Green bus on her own. She was surprised to see Kirsty scrambling on ahead of her.

"Hi!" she said. "Can I sit with you?"

Kirsty looked round and nodded.

"I didn't know you caught this bus," commented Melissa, slumping into a seat. "Do you live in Mannings Green?"

Kirsty shook her head. "No, Titchcombe," she said, naming the next village along the Cortlesham road. "But my gran does. I'm spending the night at her house. I do sometimes when things get . . ."

She stopped abruptly.

"Get what?"

"Nothing. It's just that . . ." She hesitated.

"Look," said Melissa, "you don't have to tell me anything. But maybe it would help. It's not like I'm going to tell anyone else."

"Oh everyone knows," said Kirsty with a catch in her voice. "Everyone knows and no one understands."

Melissa waited.

Kirsty glanced round the bus and dropped her voice. "About eighteen months ago, my brother got ill. Really ill."

Melissa made sympathetic noises.

"He went to hospital and had all sorts of tests and stuff and then they told us he had cancer."

Issy gasped.

Kirsty bit her lip, took a deep breath and carried on. "It was awful," she said flatly. "Tom was in hospital a lot of the time, having chemotherapy and things, but they let him home in between."

"That must have helped," said Issy, mainly because she really didn't know what else to say.

"Well, that just goes to show how little you know!" Kirsty snapped. "Oh, forget it – I don't want to talk about it!"

Issy gulped. "I'm sorry – I guess that was a pretty dumb thing to say."

Kirsty sniffed but said nothing.

"I suppose," said Melissa, trying desperately to

make amends, "that it was pretty hard watching him being ill and not being able to do anything."

"Yes, it was," replied Kirsty tightly. "Especially when you knew that your parents wished it was you who was dying."

"Dying?" Issy gasped.

"Tom died a year ago today," she replied flatly, turning to stare out of the bus window. "Two days before his sixteenth birthday."

Issy didn't know what to say. She thought about Ben and Danny. OK, Ben was a total nerd and Danny was a real pain but if either of them died . . . She shook herself. It didn't bear thinking about.

"I don't know what to say," she admitted, touching Kirsty's arm. "I mean, sorry sounds inadequate and it's pointless to say I know how you feel because I don't."

Kirsty turned and stared at her. "Do you know," she said, "that is the nicest thing anyone has said to me since it happened? Most people just tell me I should be over it by now, or say that I have to be strong for Mum and Dad."

Two tears trickled down her cheek. "I have tried to be brave, honestly I have," she said. "But I feel so guilty and so angry and – well, so alone."

Melissa frowned. "Guilty? Why?"

"I know it sounds awful but I used to get so jealous – I mean, everything centred around Tom. When he was having a good patch, Mum and Dad spent all their spare money on taking him to places he wanted to see, but when I wanted to go on the school trip to Italy they said I couldn't. I felt like I didn't matter."

Melissa frowned. "But what you just said – you know, about your parents wishing it was you and not him? They didn't really say that, did they?"

Kirsty took Melissa's handkerchief from her blazer pocket and blew her nose. "Oh no, they didn't say it – but it was pretty obvious that was what they were thinking."

Melissa stared at her. "Oh come on . . ."

"Tom was all the things that Mum and Dad ever wanted in a kid. Top in practically everything, brilliant at sport, a great trumpet player – you name it, he did it and twice as well as everyone else. He was going to follow Dad into the business and everything. Now all they've got left is thick old me."

The bus lurched round the corner into the High Street and Melissa saw that Kirsty's fists were clenched so tightly that her knuckles were white. She tried desperately to think of something comforting to say but hadn't a clue where to start. She was saved by the bus pulling into the lay-by outside The White Swan.

"Anyway," Kirsty said briskly, standing up and hoisting her schoolbag on to her shoulder, "this is my stop. My gran lives in that cottage on the corner. Will you be on the bus in the morning?"

Melissa nodded.

"See you then?"

"Sure." It sounded so feeble in comparison with all the things she wanted to say.

"I promise to be more cheerful by then," said Kirsty with a wry smile.

"You don't have to be with me, you know," replied Melissa.

"Thanks," said Kirsty solemnly. "I think you honestly mean that."

As the bus trundled on towards her stop, Melissa leaned back in her seat and thought about everything Kirsty had said. It hadn't been a fun thing to talk about and she certainly hadn't discovered much about Kirsty herself. So why was it that for the first time since leaving London, she felt as if she had found a real mate?

"Issy? Is that you, darling?"

Melissa was still doing battle with the obstinate front door as her mother's voice drifted down the hall from the kitchen. She blinked. She had been expecting a tirade of abuse but her mother sounded almost normal.

Her mother stuck her head round the kitchen door, and then squeezed through without opening it wide. Melissa could hear a scuffle from behind. If Danny had got that rat in there . . .

"Now listen," her mother began hurriedly. "There's something I want to say."

"Yes I know," sighed Melissa, sticking her tongue through the gap in her teeth the way she always did when she was in trouble. "I'm sorry about the clothes and it was only for one day, to make a point, and I won't do it again. Well, not much of it, anyway."

The skirt was somewhat beyond redemption.

"Oh that. Yes, well I can't say I approve, but I see you've removed the worst of the damage, and I expect the school have had their say."

Is that it? thought Melissa. I needn't have gone so overboard in my humility.

"Right now, I've got more important things on my mind and I need your help."

In Melissa's brain, warning bells started ringing most alarmingly. "I am not singing in the choir and that is final," she declared. "You can shove Danny into a surplice and let him con people into thinking he's angelic, but leave me out of it."

Her mother shook her head. "It's not that," she said. "Anyway, before I say any more come into the kitchen. I've got a surprise."

Five minutes later, after the surprise had leaped at Melissa with unrestrained joy, licked her from head to toe, offered her a rather chewed slipper and then collapsed, panting, on to the floor, Melissa threw her arms round her mother and gave her a hug.

"And I really can keep him?" she demanded for the third time. "You won't change your mind?"

"Of course not," said her mother. "But you'll have to make sure he doesn't go near Danny's beloved rat."

"Barnaby," said Melissa, "has far too much sense to go anywhere near that manic child. What was it you wanted me to help with?"

Now that her mother had been so brilliant over

Barnaby, Melissa was prepared to scale Everest in flip-flops to show her gratitude.

"I'm starting a youth group here at St Peter's," Fay announced, watching Melissa carefully.

"That's nice," said Issy, patting Barnaby's head.

"And I thought you could ask some of your friends along for the first . . ."

"Oh no!" Melissa stared at her mother, open-mouthed. "No way! I've just about managed to get in with the gang – do you honestly think I'm going to drag them along to some goody-goody youth club?"

Her mother tried to look hip and happening. "Oh, heavens, no!" she said. "It's not going to be your normal, run-of-the-mill thing. It's going to be just for the over-fourteens, really trendy, ground-breaking stuff and . . ."

"Well, that's fine," interjected Issy. "You go and break ground with someone else and leave me out of it, OK? It's hard enough having to live down a holy holy image at school without you wanting to thrust religion down my friends. Especially when it's meaningless."

"Melissa!" Fay stared at her. She knew that Issy was not wholly convinced of her mother's sanity but she had never really challenged Fay on the basics. "Of course it's not meaningless."

"Well, tell that to Kirsty!" retorted Melissa.

"Kirsty?"

"She's my new friend," said Melissa.

"Darling, that's lovely . ."

"If God is so wonderful, how come he let her brother die when he was only sixteen? Answer me that!"

"Oh." Fay sat down at the kitchen table and took hold of one of Melissa's hands. "I don't know, darling."

"What do you mean, you don't know? You're supposed to be a priest, aren't you?"

Her mother nodded. "Yes, but that doesn't mean I have all the answers. I wish I did – it's hard, when someone dies, to know what to say to the people left behind."

Melissa nodded. "That's just it," she said. "I don't think I said any of the right things. And somehow I get the feeling . . ."

She paused.

"What feeling?"

"I guess she feels really alone," said Melissa.

"Perhaps you could bring her along to this new youth group . . ."

Melissa jumped up. "You are unreal! Going to some dippy club isn't going to help anything. Besides . . ."

"What?"

"Nothing. By the way, I'm going to London next weekend. OK?"

Fay frowned. "What for?"

"Shopping. With some of my mates."

Her mum looked at her eager face and decided not to comment on the fact that, according to Melissa, she was never going to have a single mate ever again.

"Sounds lovely, darling," she said. "Is Kirsty going?"

"No," said Melissa. "Well, yes, maybe." She hadn't thought of that. It might cheer her up and take her mind off things.

"So could you sub me some money? Just till my next allowance? Please?"

"If I do, will you think about the youth club?"

Issy looked at her mother in mock horror. "Mum! That's bribery! How unholy!"

"So?" said her mother with a grin. "I never said I was perfect. Now go walk your dog."

"Hey, it's the angry ant!"

Melissa turned to see Matt Carter jumping from the Cortlesham College bus and grinning at her.

"Pardon?"

"Small, cross, but very determined!" he grinned. "Still attempting to master the art of dog-walking, I see!"

Melissa grinned despite herself. "He's mine now," she said proudly. "I've adopted him."

She expected some sarcastic remark but Matt looked impressed. "Cool," he said. "Does this mean I get to see you struggling your way round the village on a regular basis?"

"Depends whether you're looking," replied Melissa coolly.

"Oh, I'll be looking," he said more softly, his milk chocolate eyes staring straight into hers. He stretched out a hand and flicked a strand of ginger hair from her eyes.

Barnaby looked away in embarrassment.

Melissa's stomach decided to relocate itself somewhere to the left of her heart.

"I can't wait," said Matt. "See you!"

And with that, he walked off in the opposite direction without a backward glance.

Melissa watched him go and then tugged on Barnaby's lead.

"He said he couldn't wait!" she told him. "He said he'd be looking. Do you think he fancies me?"

Barnaby gave her a blank look.

"No, you're probably right," she sighed. "He was probably just winding me up. But he is cute, isn't he? Those eyes and his . . ."

There is only so much sloppy talk a self-respecting crossbreed can take. Spotting an aristocratic-looking Siamese cat dozing on a nearby stone wall, Barnaby gave two authoritative barks, changed gear and began chasing the unsuspecting feline at such speed that all thoughts of possible passion were swiftly removed from Melissa's mind.

CHAPTER NINE
GUILTY SECRETS

HUGO WOKE UP ON FRIDAY morning with a thundering headache and a sick feeling in the pit of his stomach. The headache was due largely to the champagne and claret he had drunk the night before; the sick feeling was undiluted guilt.

How had it happened? He had never meant it to go that far. He had met Joanna for a drink at a wine bar and then suggested a Thai meal. Just to help her with her project. Even after the meal, when they had been strolling along the Embankment and somehow his hand had slipped into Joanna's and stayed there, he had told himself that he was merely being supportive to a young girl who had just opened her heart to him.

"I don't want to be part of the money-making rat race," she had said, gazing up at him with those incredible slate-grey eyes. "I want to do some good, make a difference."

And all the time she had been telling him about the houses she wanted to design for the disabled, and how she dreamed of going to South America and converting disused buildings into centres for street children, he had been mesmerised by her ivory skin and the way she held her head to one side when she got animated.

And then she had shivered in the rapidly cooling

May evening air, and he had said why didn't they go back to his place for a coffee and Cognac and she had said yes. And they had sat for a long time, talking. And then not talking. And then . . .

Hugo shook his head. It must never ever happen again. He must make it quite clear to her today that it had been a big mistake, that he was a happily married man and that they mustn't see one another any more.

But she made him feel so alive, so young. He loved her enthusiasm, her desire to do good. And yes, if he was honest, he loved the way she idolised him, told him he was the most attractive man she had ever met. Not to see her again would be . . . but he mustn't. He would go to his meeting, catch the train home and put the whole episode behind him. It must never happen again.

No way. Not ever again.

Issy pushed her way to the back of the bus, where Ellie and Tara, who'd been poring over the new issue of *Heaven Sent* magazine, were beckoning to her furiously.

"Hi!" said Melissa, slumping into her seat. "TGIF!"

"Pardon?" said Tara.

"Thank God It's Friday, silly," interpreted Ellie, grabbing the handrail as the bus jolted away from the stop. "Are you seeing Matt Carter at the weekend?"

"Maybe," replied Melissa non-committally, pushing her purple beret to an even more jaunty angle. It was obvious that Ellie thought they were some sort of item and she was not about to pass up the opportunity of increasing her social standing by confessing to having only spoken to him a few times. "Why?"

"Ask him along to my party, why don't you?" suggested Ellie eagerly, thrusting a couple of invitations into her hand. "That would be really cool. For you, I mean," she added hastily as Tara gave her a quizzical look.

"Thanks," said Melissa. Not that there was any way she could ask him. He was bound to have a girlfriend and besides, he was too tall. And full of himself. She would just have to come up with some excuse.

Thankfully, the bus pulled up at The White Swan and she was able to avoid an answer. "Hey, there's Kirsty!" she said. "Hi!"

Ellie and Tara looked up in surprise.

"She doesn't usually get this bus," commented Tara.

"She's been staying at her grandmother's house," explained Melissa. "She does sometimes."

Kirsty sank down into the only remaining seat at the front of the bus and mouthed a greeting to Melissa.

"How come you know so much? She's not a mate of yours, is she?" asked Ellie.

"Yes," said Melissa. "Well, I only met her yesterday but . . ."

"You don't want to get involved with her," said

Tara. "She's an awful drip."

"That's not fair!" said Melissa defensively. "She's had a really rough time. You probably don't know, but her brother died of cancer."

"Oh, I know," said Tara. "But that was ages ago. She should have got over it by now."

"And it wasn't like it was a big shock or anything," said Ellie. "I mean, he'd been ill for months and everyone knew that he'd probably die."

Melissa was about to protest but thought better of it. "Is she coming to your party?" she ventured.

"Oh *please*!" Ellie looked at her in horror. "My party's for the cool crowd and she is definitely not it. Say, how do you think I'd look in that?"

She stabbed a purple-varnished finger at the centrefold of her magazine and indicated a sugar-pink chiffon slip dress.

"Like a stick of candyfloss," giggled Tara.

Melissa said nothing. She had worked so hard to get accepted by Ellie and that lot, and now she was considered one of the cool crowd, which was great. But she really liked Kirsty as well and she guessed that right now Kirsty needed a friend. The trouble was that if she spent too much time with her, Ellie and Tara would probably block her out.

Of course, she could have it both ways. She could hang out and have a laugh with Ellie's crowd at school and spend time having more serious conversations and heart-to-hearts with Kirsty when they weren't around.

That would be the way to play it. That way, she would have the best of both worlds.

While Melissa was planning her social strategy, her elder brother was perched on the wall outside Cortlesham College, putting the finishing touches to his A level computing assignment.

"Don't tell me you've finished it?"

A pungent aroma of flowery perfume enveloped him. He looked up to see Vicki Landcross, chest protruding from an exceedingly tight black Lycra body, eyeing his homework in awe.

"I, er, yes," he began, his heart thundering in his chest. She was so – lovely.

"You're so clever," she sighed, flicking her black hair over her shoulder. "I'm totally stuck – what does it mean?"

She leaned over him, her hair lightly brushing his cheek. He thought he might faint. "Show me – please?" she said huskily.

"It's dead easy," Ben gabbled. "You have to distinguish between serial and parallel transmission. I'll show you."

Ten minutes later, his palms damp with sweat from her continued proximity, he closed the book. "And that's all there is to it really," he said, wishing there was more.

"I get it!" said Vicki, beaming broadly. "Ben Bailey, you're an angel!"

And she planted a kiss on his cheek. "Must dash,"

she said. "Sociology in five minutes. Catch you for a coffee at lunch-time! Yes?"

Ben swallowed. "Well, er – yes, OK."

"Great! Ciao!"

Ben stared after her, as she ran lightly towards the main entrance, and touched his cheek as if in a trance.

A girl had kissed him. Well, not kissed exactly. More pecked. But it was a start.

For a moment he felt almost normal. And then his heart sank. She may have kissed him. But he hadn't kissed her. And he couldn't. He'd be bound to get it wrong. That time with Tanya – she'd laughed and said he was a right amateur.

He wasn't going to risk that happening again.

But Vicki was lovely.

And they were going to have coffee at lunch-time.

For now he would just think about that.

Hugo knew he should have been thinking about the design for the mezzanine floor of the new Internet café but somehow a vision of Joanna, face upturned to his, kept drifting in front of his drawing board. It had been the same during the meeting; he'd heard the business with half an ear, while the rest of his mind kept replaying the way she had said "I think I love you".

It was no good. This was insanity. Tossing his pencil aside, he picked up his briefcase, strode across the office and stuck his head round his partner's door.

"I'm leaving early, Roger," he said. "Bit of a headache."

"OK, old boy," said Roger. "Can't say I blame you; going home to the country air, wife, kids . . ." His voice trailed off. Roger was divorced, childless and lived with his elderly mother in Ruislip.

"Quite," said Hugo, desperately trying to suppress the pang of guilt that threatened to swamp him.

At Victoria station he bought a large bunch of carnations and a box of Fay's favourite mint chocolates.

From the phone box at Cortlesham station he booked a table for two at The Drunken Chicken.

And into the waste bin beside the taxi rank he threw the receipt for last night's dinner.

It was over. It would be as if it had never happened.

CHAPTER TEN
JUST DO THIS AND I'LL ALWAYS BE GOOD!

"WELCOME TO OUR WORSHIP this morning. We begin by singing hymn number 327 in *Mission Praise*, 'Immortal invisible, God only wise'. "

Fay Bailey picked up her hymn book, threw a warning glance at Danny who was standing with the trebles making paper darts from his order of service sheet, and began to sing.

She felt good. Everything was at last beginning to fall into place. Melissa hadn't complained about Mannings Green for three whole days, which had to be an all time record; Ben had actually spent Saturday in town instead of stuck in front of that wretched computer, and Danny's riding-school instructor had told her that he was a natural and a joy to teach. It would be nice if the staff of the village school felt the same, but at least it was a step in the right direction.

They'd had a pretty good weekend so far. To be honest, she had been dreading Hugo's reaction when he discovered that in his absence the family unit had swelled by two and he now had to share a house he didn't like with a manic dog and a large white rat – but he had taken it like a lamb, even dumping Danny in the car and whisking him off to Pet City for a cage there and then. Of course, he had forgotten all about going to John Lewis for the fabric but he'd explained that the pressure of work had been enormous and she hadn't the heart to say she was pretty busy too. He had seemed a bit depressed when she told him he couldn't knock down walls in a house that didn't belong to them, but then he had presented her with flowers and chocolates and they had gone out for dinner, where he had even held her hand across the table, something he hadn't done in years.

"If I didn't know you better," she had teased him over the crêpes Suzette, "I'd say you had a guilty secret."

"Don't be so silly!" Hugo had snapped and she had kissed his fingers and told him she was only joking.

On Saturday, they had all gone for a walk to watch Danny ride and, apart from the worrying moment when Barnaby had assumed that if the ponies were jumping hurdles he could too, it had been a great success.

And now, just to prove miracles could happen, her entire family was in church. It gave her a warm glow to look at them: Danny in his white surplice looking, misleadingly, like a small angel; Melissa, dressed for the catwalk admittedly, but at least wearing a smile; and Ben, face screwed in concentration, singing words which, for one who attended church only when his mother threatened to disconnect his computer if he didn't, were somewhat unfamiliar. And Hugo – dear Hugo, who couldn't sing a note and mouthed the words like a puppet out of sequence with the organ.

'All laud we would render: O help us to see
'tis only the splendour of light hideth thee.'

The organ fell silent. Fay smiled expansively at the expectant congregation. "Let us pray," she said.

". . . so God, if you are there, like Mum says, can you help Kirsty? She says it's really awful at home because her mum's on pills and really spaced out and her dad keeps pushing her to work harder and get better grades like Tom did. I don't know what you can do but you're supposed to be all-powerful so could you get on with it and cheer her up?

Oh and can I be totally zit-free for Saturday? And find a suede miniskirt I can afford for Ellie's party? Thanks a lot. Amen."

"Forgive me. Please. Just forgive me. Help me to stop thinking about her. Please. Or find her a job in Scotland or something. Anything to take the temptation away. Amen."

"God bless Mum and Dad and Ben and make Issy be nicer to Humphrey and please can you make me understand compound interest and those fraction things and please please please please make Mum and Dad get me my own pony. Soon. Amen.

PS That was Danny speaking. Thanks. Amen."

"Just don't let anyone find that book in my room, God, OK? *Supercool With The Opposite Sex* – that one. I suppose you don't approve of that kind of stuff but it's my last hope. I mean, I can't talk to Dad about – well, you know – because he and Mum have been together for so long, I bet he's forgotten what it's like to really, really fancy someone.

That dream I had last night, the one where I kissed Vicki and she told me that I was the coolest guy she knew? Make it come true, God. Soon. Amen."

Melissa got up from her knees and sat back in the pew, as the choir stood up to sing the anthem. This was where the boring bits began and she had just started to pick bits of silver polish off her thumbnail when the heavy oak door at the south end of the church creaked and the big iron latch clattered, just in the quietest part of the singing.

Mr Haverstock, the churchwarden, bustled over importantly, laying a finger to his lips and shushing as a small figure slipped into the church and glanced anxiously around. Melissa's mouth dropped open. It was Kirsty.

"Over here!" she whispered. From the pew in front, Mrs Cumberforth-Jones turned round and glared.

"What are you doing here?" hissed Melissa as Kirsty slid in beside her.

"Looking for you," muttered Kirsty. "I was bored – and curious, I guess!"

"Will you two be quiet!" Mrs C-J's chest heaved alarmingly.

"Sorry," said Melissa meekly and pulled a face behind Mrs Cumberforth-Jones's back.

"Is that your mum?" mouthed Kirsty as the anthem ended and Mrs Bailey mounted the steps into the carved pulpit.

"Yes," said Melissa reluctantly and began praying that her mother would keep it short, sweet and, most importantly of all, totally without embarrassment.

"I want," began her mother, "to talk to you today about the young."

So much, thought Melissa, for the power of prayer.

CHAPTER ELEVEN
SOCIAL STRATEGIES

"THIS IS KIRSTY, MUM." Melissa gestured towards her friend as they filed through the church porch where Mrs Bailey was shaking the hands of her congregation.

"Hi," said Kirsty shyly.

"How nice to see you here!" beamed Fay. "And I do hope I shall see you at the new youth group I was talking about – of course, Issy . . ."

"Mum, don't go on!" hissed Melissa, shoving Kirsty past her. "Kirsty doesn't even live in Mannings Green."

"Makes no difference, darling, it will be open to anyone," said her mother easily, as a small, pale-faced woman gripped her hand. "Ah, Mrs Frobisher, so glad to see you up and about again."

"Come on," said Melissa quickly, grabbing the opportunity. "Let's go."

"Take your friend over to the hall for coffee," called Fay, trying desperately to release her hand. "I'll catch you there."

Oh please, thought Melissa, crossing the road. On a scale of one to ten for entertainment value, that ranked about minus five.

"I guess you've got to get home, haven't you?" she asked.

Kirsty shook her head. "That's the last thing I want to do," she admitted. "Mum and Dad go to the cemetery on Sunday mornings and they always try to drag me along."

"And you don't want to go?"

Kirsty shook her head. "I just can't face it. I'd rather remember . . ." Her voice trailed off and she gave herself a little shake. "So coffee would be fine."

"No," said Melissa rapidly. "We'll go back to my house and . . ."

She stopped. She had just remembered. She couldn't possibly take Kirsty home, not now. Not today.

"No, I know, we'll take Barnaby – he's my dog – for a walk. That way we can talk in private. OK?"

"Sure," agreed Kirsty with a grin. "Whatever you like."

". . . and that new single by Paper Turkey is so wicked, don't you think?"

"You really like it? Me too!"

Melissa tugged on Barnaby's lead in a vain attempt to stop him playing touch football with an empty Coke can that was blowing around in the wind. She and Kirsty had already circled the village four times talking non-stop about everything from which were the most fanciable groups in the charts to the fact that half the teachers at Furze Grange were total dinosaurs.

"I'm really glad we're going to be friends," said Kirsty now as they crossed the village green on the way to her bus stop. "It's just a pity we're not in the same class, isn't it?"

"Yes," said Melissa, thinking that if they were, it would be a lot harder to keep their friendship a secret from Ellie and the others. "Still, you must have heaps of friends in 10W, haven't you?" she asked.

Kirsty shrugged. "I did have," she admitted. "But somehow when Tom died, most of them kind of drifted. Whenever I wanted to talk about Tom, they changed the subject and started going on about rock concerts or clothes – as if he wasn't important at all."

Melissa murmured sympathetically. She felt sorry for Kirsty but she could see how it must have been for her friends. She didn't know what to say now – so it must have been heaps harder just after it all happened.

"Anyway, now I've got you," said Kirsty happily. "And there's this new youth club we can go to . . ."

"You have to be kidding?"

"Why? Your mum said she had some really cool ideas."

"My mother's idea of cool is in fact very lukewarm," said Issy firmly.

Kirsty shrugged. "OK, but why don't we spend Saturday together – we could go shopping or catch a movie or . . ."

Melissa thought fast. If she told Kirsty about the London trip she would want to come along too, and Ellie would flip.

"I can't," she said. "We've – we've got visitors."

Kirsty's face fell.

"But we could go out one evening in the week," said Issy quickly.

Kirsty shook her head. "I'm not allowed," she said. "To quote my father, 'If you're going to do as well as Tom you need to apply yourself.' I just can't get him to see that it isn't going to happen."

She sighed. "Anyway, I guess I'd better be getting back, there aren't so many buses back to Titchcombe on a Sunday. I'll see you at school, OK?"

"Sure," said Melissa.

"And you can tell me the times of this youth club, right?"

Wrong, thought Melissa, eyeing her in alarm. Kirsty didn't seriously think that a group run by her mother was going to be anything but totally dire, did she?

Maybe Ellie was right; maybe Kirsty was rather sad.

Which was all the more reason for keeping quiet about the fact that despite all that, she really did like her a lot.

It didn't prove as easy as Melissa had hoped. For one thing, every lunch-time Kirsty would appear at the table where she was sitting with Ellie and Tara and a bunch of other kids in her class and hover, waiting for someone to move up and make a space on the bench. On Monday, Issy wriggled closer to Tara and gestured to Kirsty to sit down – and then felt awful when the others spent the whole meal talking about Ellie's party and which guys they were going to pull and ignored Kirsty completely. On Tuesday, she got up and went to sit with Kirsty at another table, but was so busy straining her ears to hear what the others were talking about that she didn't concentrate on anything Kirsty was saying.

On Wednesday it all came to a head. Ellie had grabbed Issy's arm the moment they sat down.

"Well, is he coming or not?"

Melissa blinked.

"Matt, silly. You have asked him, haven't you?"

Melissa gulped. She didn't want to admit to the fact that she hadn't seen him for days, never mind invited him to a party. "He's going to let me know," she lied. "He's got a couple of things to sort."

"But he's keen?" Ellie urged.

"Oh yes, ever so keen," said Issy.

"Who's keen?" Kirsty appeared at her elbow, balancing a tray.

For once, Ellie deigned to acknowledge Kirsty's presence. "Matt Carter – Issy's boyfriend," she said.

Kirsty stared at Melissa. "You never told me you had a boyfriend," she said.

That was primarily because I don't, thought Issy.

"So?" interjected Tara, tossing her brown braid over her shoulder. "What makes you think she'd tell you her private business, anyway? You only talk about that kind of stuff with your mates."

Kirsty dropped her eyes.

"It's no big deal," began Melissa, but Kirsty had already moved away.

"What did you have to go and say that for?" demanded Issy.

"Well, we are your mates, aren't we?"

"Yes, but so is . . . yes, yes, of course you are."

Melissa didn't see Kirsty after school that day, because she had drama club, and on Thursday Mrs Fisher, who was obviously suffering from a very bad dose of pre-menstrual tension combined with a total lack of humour, spent so long at the end of French telling her that she wouldn't get anywhere in life without a grasp of the past participle that all her friends had eaten lunch and dispersed into the school field by the time Melissa reached the canteen. It wasn't until Thursday afternoon, as she ambled across the school yard to the gate, that she caught up with Kirsty.

"Am I glad to see you!" she began.

"Really?" Kirsty sounded cool and disbelieving.

"Of course," affirmed Issy as they walked through the gates to the bus stop. "Look, about yesterday – Tara was well out of order."

Kirsty shrugged. "It's OK," she said curtly. "I mean, you don't know me, do you? You might think I'd want to steal this boyfriend of yours."

"That's crazy – of course I wouldn't!"

"Why? Don't you think I'm attractive enough?"

"Of course you are, you're stunning! Oh, this is ridiculous!"

Melissa turned to face her. "Look, Matt Carter – he's not my boyfriend!"

Kirsty frowned. "But Ellie said . . ."

"Yes, well – look, if I tell you the truth, can you promise to keep quiet about it?"

Kirsty nodded.

"Ellie and Tara think that Matt and I are an item, but we're not. I've only spoken to him about three times and even then all he does is take the mickey. The trouble is . . ."

She cast a wary glance over her shoulder and dropped her voice. ". . . Ellie told me to invite him to her party and now she keeps pestering me to know whether he's coming."

"And you haven't asked him yet?" queried Kirsty, picking up her bag as the Titchcombe bus came round the corner.

"Yet? I can't ask him – I've just told you that I hardly know the guy."

"But you like him?"

"No – well, yes – yes, he's quite cute," she admitted.

"And you wouldn't object to going out with him?"

"No – but . . ."

"So go for it," insisted Kirsty, as the bus pulled up. "Ask the guy."

"And what if he just laughs and says no?"

Kirsty shrugged. "You will be no worse off, will you? Where does he live?"

Melissa frowned. "I don't know," she admitted. "Somewhere in the village. I see him around from time to time. Anyway, even if I saw him, what would I say? I can't do it – it's crazy!"

"I can see that you need the advice of an older woman," teased Kirsty, who was exactly three weeks older than Issy. "I'll come round to your house after school tomorrow – I'm spending the night with my gran anyway. We'll get it sorted."

"You can't, I . . ." began Melissa trying desperately to think of a reason to stop Kirsty coming to five Church Hill.

"Oh yes I can," said Kirsty, stepping on to the bus and waving. "After all, that's what friends are for!"

And with that the bus pulled away before Melissa had time to reply.

She couldn't put Kirsty off. She would hurt her feelings again and she didn't want to do that.

She'd just have to make sure that things at home were sorted before Kirsty turned up.

"Ben?"

"Uh-huh?"

"What are you doing tomorrow after college?"

"Coming home I suppose. Why?"

"So you're not going into town or anything?"

"No."

"Oh."

"Danny?"

"Yup?"

"Do you want to earn fifty pence?"

"You bet!"

"Right – this is what you have to do."

Melissa leaned forward and whispered in her brother's ear.

"That's worth a pound at least!"

"Seventy-five pence and that's my final offer."

"You're on!"

There were times, thought Melissa, when small brothers had their uses.

CHAPTER TWELVE
LIES, BRIBES AND LET-DOWNS

"IT'S REALLY JUST TO SAY thank you."

Hugo pressed the lift button and stared at the envelope which Joanna had slipped into his hand. Just five minutes earlier, he had been congratulating himself on getting to Friday morning without seeing her again. Admittedly, she had been out of the office on a course all week, but he had resisted the temptation to pick up the phone and invite her out to dinner, and he had even managed to go for a whole hour at a time without thinking about her.

And now he was in an empty lift with her, conscious

of her eyes watching him as he ripped open the envelope.

He pulled out two tickets for the new production of *Madam Butterfly*.

"Joanna! These are like gold dust – how did you do it?"

She smiled. "You said you'd love to see it," she said. "And I wanted to make you happy."

She moved nearer to him. "As happy as you make me."

Her lips brushed his cheek.

His throat tightened. He couldn't go. Obviously. The performance was for tonight. Friday May the twentieth. He was due to catch the 5.11 p.m. train home.

"I know it's awfully short notice," Joanna said, as if reading his mind. "But to get dress circle seats was a miracle and that was all they had."

"I – I don't know, I . . ."

Joanna blinked and allowed her hand to brush his. "Of course," she said, with a crack in her voice. "It was stupid of me. You'll have much better things to do – I'll take someone else."

Hugo stared into her grey eyes. He didn't want her to take anyone else. He couldn't even bear to think that she might have someone else to take.

It wouldn't matter so much if he went out that evening and caught a really early train home on Saturday morning. He'd still have the whole weekend with the family. After all, there was no harm in an evening at the opera. And that was all it would be. Just that.

"Joanna, I'd love to come," he smiled, as the lift clanked to a halt on the twenty-eighth floor, and was rewarded with a dazzling smile.

He touched her cheek then withdrew his hand sharply as the lift doors opened to reveal three of his colleagues waiting patiently in the corridor.

"Seven thirty in the bar?" queried Joanna.

"Fine," he said. "Absolutely fine."

"Fay? Hugo. How are you, darling? Terrific. Look, sweetheart, it's an awful bore but I'm going to have to stay up here tonight. You remember the Internet café project? Well the client is insisting on dinner and a chat before he flies off on holiday. I know, me too – but I'll be home mid-morning. Of course I promise. All right, darling, see you then. Love to the kids. Bye!"

Fay kicked off her shoes, poured a second cup of tea and contemplated the day ahead. Friday was her day off, and if anyone in the parish gave birth, felt peeved, died or lost the keys to the vestry, it was Donald's problem and not hers. And she had so been looking forward to Hugo coming home early, to cooking him a special meal and then maybe persuading him to go and see that new film at the Virgin cinema in Cortlesham. And now he had to work. She thought it was a bit much that clients should expect him to cut into his weekend; she'd have to tell him to say no in future. That was the thing about Hugo – he couldn't say no.

Still, she thought, there were worse things than a man who was dedicated to his job. She should be thankful that he was so hardworking – after all, they couldn't live on the money she earned.

"It's going to be such a cool weekend!" Ellie said at lunch-time. "I've made this ginormous list of gear I want to get in London – I even persuaded the parents to cough up with an early birthday pressie! Fifty quid!"

"Wow!" said Tara. "All I got out of my mum was the train fare and a long lecture about not blowing my allowance because money doesn't grow on trees. What about you, Issy?"

"Pardon?" Melissa had been thinking rather more about the coming afternoon than the trip to London. The latter was going to be a doddle; she was far more worried about just what Kirsty had in mind regarding Matt Carter and whether Danny would do as he promised and prevent a disaster at teatime.

"Are you all ready for tomorrow?" demanded Ellie. "You know what train and everything?"

Melissa nodded.

"The 9.10 from Cortlesham," she said.

"Well, don't miss it," ordered Ellie. "We don't want anything to mess up the day."

"Nothing will," said Melissa. "Trust me, nothing will."

Ben walked across the college quadrangle in a daze. He'd done it. He'd asked her out. And, even more amazing, she had said yes. And to think that only a week ago he was scared at the thought of having a cup of coffee with her.

Actually, he was still a bit scared. She was so – knowledgeable. She talked about all the other guys she had dated and gave them marks out of ten.

"No one ever got beyond seven and a half," she had breathed, leaning her head on his shoulder and sending shivers down his spine. "But I guess you'll hit the jackpot, Benjy."

Normally Ben would decapitate anyone who called him that, but somehow the way she had linked her arms round the back of his neck and pouted her lips at him took up his concentration to such an extent that he hardly noticed.

"So," she had continued, running an immaculately manicured fingernail under his chin, while he prayed she wouldn't find the zit that had erupted that very morning, "shall I pick you up?"

"Pardon?"

"I passed my driving test last week," she had said proudly. "I can borrow my dad's car. I'll be round at seven."

Ben had frowned. It wouldn't do his macho image one bit of good to be seen being driven by a girl. But then again, what with paying for drinks and maybe a pizza, he'd be strapped for cash if he had to lash out for a cab as well so he had said yes.

And now he just wanted the next lecture to be over so that he could get home and shower and sort out his clothes and borrow his dad's aftershave.

He had to get this right. His whole future depended on it.

"Right," said Kirsty as the school bus trundled along the main road towards Mannings Green. "This is what we do. We go to your house, you get changed, we get Barnaby and walk over to Matt's house . . ."

"But I told you," protested Melissa, "I don't know where he lives."

"Fourteen Spinney Rise," said Kirsty with a grin.

"And how did you find that out?"

"Easy," her friend replied. "I asked my gran if she knew anyone by the name of Carter in the village. Turns out she knows Matt's mum through the WI."

Melissa was impressed. "But we can't just ring the doorbell and say, 'Hey, do you want to come to a party?', can we?" she protested.

"That's where Barnaby comes in," said Kirsty. "Leave it to me. I've got it all sussed. All you have to do is dress to kill."

"Oh Melissa dear, here you are and me just waxed my floor so you'll have to keep out of the kitchen and my, you've brought a little friend back, that's nice."

Connie, swathed in a purple pinafore and wearing a

pair of bright yellow rubber gloves at least two sizes too large, beamed at them.

"Your mum's gone to get her hair done, and bless her, she deserves a treat, what with all that she does for the village. I was only saying to Mrs Frobisher when I saw her at the doctor's – it was my feet again, dear – 'Mrs Frobisher,' I said, 'that reverend is a sainted woman,' and she said . . ."

"That's great, Connie," interrupted Melissa in desperation, as Kirsty spluttered behind her hand. "And where's Danny?"

"Dashed out a few minutes ago, said he was on a secret mission, bless him."

Great, thought Issy. For once he's doing as he's told. It's going to be OK.

"Come on," she said to Kirsty. "Let's see if your plan really does work."

"Ben! Ben! Come quickly – it's an emergency!"

Danny was rather impressed by his theatrical performance.

His brother stepped off the bus and ambled straight past him as if he was invisible.

"Ben! There's been a crisis!"

Ben turned, blinked and peered at Danny. "What crisis?"

"It's Mum – the car's broken down and she sent me to get you because you understand mechanical stuff."

Ben glanced at his watch. In two hours' time Vicki

would be arriving and he had to shower and change. He couldn't be doing with incompetent mothers right now.

"Can't she phone the AA or something? That's what they are there for," he said.

"No," said Danny firmly. "She said you had to come. At once. Follow me."

He set off at a rapid trot and reluctantly Ben followed.

At least it would be good practice in case Vicki's car broke down. Women were always so useless in a crisis.

"Oh my gosh, it's him. Look, over there. Don't look!"

Melissa stood stock-still in the middle of the pavement.

"What do you mean, don't look? I can hardly sort your love life with my eyes closed."

Kirsty peered down the road to where Matt Carter was emerging from the gate of one of the green-roofed bungalows.

"What, that guy on the skateboard? Very fit! No wonder you're impressed."

"I'm not. Particularly," said Melissa.

"Oh no, of course not. OK, let's go." Kirsty took Barnaby's lead from Melissa's hand, unclipped it from his collar and knelt down beside him.

"Barnaby, off you go!"

Barnaby threw her an astonished look. Leads only came off in the recreation ground or the fields.

"Go, you stupid mongrel!"

Barnaby went.

"Kirsty, are you mad? We'll never catch him now – he's like a greyhound when the mood takes him!"

"Precisely," said Kirsty. "Watch."

Barnaby was hurtling down the road, executing occasional three-point turns in the air and snapping at his own tail. When he spotted Matt boarding along ahead of him, he accelerated up a gear and, with a joyous bark, threw himself at the back wheels.

Matt wobbled, swore, wobbled again and fell off.

"Now!" hissed Kirsty. "Just look sort of concerned and loving and guilty and yet somehow remote and alluring."

"Oh is that all?" said Issy. And then, noticing that Barnaby was endeavouring to lick Matt to death, she ran down the road.

"I'm really, really sorry," she said. "Are you OK?"

Matt struggled to his feet, brushing dust off his jeans. "Yes, no thanks to you," he said, looming over Issy and looking exceedingly cross. "I told you that dog was too much for you."

"He is not!" retorted Melissa.

Kirsty panted up behind her. "It's not Melissa's fault," she said sweetly, her eyes scanning Matt's face. "It's all mine. She warned me not to let him off the lead, but I wouldn't listen. Issy is so sensible. But very fun-loving too," she added hastily.

Melissa cringed. "Are you sure you're not hurt?" she said.

"I'll live," acknowledged Matt, breaking into a grin. "But you owe me one."

Kirsty nudged her in the ribs. "Go on," she hissed.

Melissa opened her mouth and then shut it again.

"What my friend is trying to say is that there is this amazing party with a disco and everything and she wants you to go along with her."

Matt raised an eyebrow and busied himself with flicking the skateboard with his foot. "Yeah?" he mumbled.

Melissa studied the cracks in the pavement with great interest.

"I don't know that I dare risk it," he said, jumping on to the board.

Melissa's heart sank, but she shrugged as if she couldn't care less.

"I mean," he said, "are you as dangerous when you are dancing as when you are dog-walking?"

Issy looked up. Matt's eyes were twinkling but his face was dead serious.

"You going to this party?" Matt asked Kirsty.

Kirsty shook her head.

"That good, eh?" grinned Matt. "See you around, kiddos!" And with that, he boarded off.

Melissa turned to Kirsty, who was gazing after Matt.

"See?" she said truculently. "I told you it wouldn't work. Now he'll think I'm a total idiot."

Kirsty shook her head. "You really are thick, aren't you?" she said.

"I beg your pardon?"

"It's obvious he was really chuffed," she said.

"He was?"

"Of course," affirmed Kirsty. "All you have to do is keep looking as if you couldn't care less."

"Which I couldn't," said Issy.

"Of course you couldn't," said Kirsty.

"So where is the car?" demanded Ben for the fourth time. They had walked right through the village and were headed towards Titchcombe.

Danny decided he had pushed his luck far enough. "Nowhere," he said.

"*Nowhere?*" expostulated Ben.

"It was a trick," said Danny.

"It was what?" Ben loomed over him, his hands reaching out as if to wring his neck.

"It wasn't my idea," insisted Danny. "It was Issy's. She paid me."

"Don't give me that!"

"She did, honestly. She said she'd got this friend coming and she wanted you out of the way and she'd give me seventy-five pence if I'd keep you out of the house for as long as possible."

"Right," said Ben. "Just wait till I get my hands on her."

He turned and began striding back towards the village centre.

Danny trotted after him.

This he had to see.

They were halfway home when a tall guy on a skateboard called out to Ben.

"Hi there!" he said. "How's the love life?"

Danny, who had been lagging behind, talking to one of the ponies in the riding-school field, pricked his ears up.

"Shut up!" retorted Ben.

"I hear you and the glorious Vicki are now an item," persisted Matt. "So you finally got your act together?"

"What is it to you?" said Ben.

"I was thinking of moving in there myself, you know," said Matt. "So if you can't stand the pace . . ."

"Oh go boil your head!" snapped Ben.

Matt grinned and skated off.

"Are you in love?" asked Danny, wrinkling his nose as if he had just discovered that his older brother was into swimming in silage.

"Mind your own business!" said Ben.

"Which means you are," reasoned Danny. "I'm going to tell Melissa."

He began running ahead of Ben, chanting, "Ben's in love, sexy sexy Ben. Ben's in love, sexy sexy . . ."

"Danny, shut up! If you dare say a word to anyone . . ."

Danny stopped. "What's it worth?"

Ben glared at him.

"Well?"

"You can't blackmail me," said his brother loftily.

"OK," said Danny equably. "Ben's in love, sexy, sexy . . ."

"Fifty pence," said Ben.

"One pound," said Danny.

"Total and complete silence?"

Danny nodded.

"Done," said Ben.

CHAPTER THIRTEEN
CONFESSIONS AND CONFIDENCES

"IT'S LOVELY TO SEE YOU, Kirsty," said Mrs Bailey, putting a large pizza on the table and offering Kirsty a slice.

"Thanks!" said Kirsty. "It's great to be here."

"And are you part of tomorrow's great expedition?"

Kirsty frowned. "Excuse me?" she said, looking puzzled.

Melissa was trying desperately to think of a way to change the subject when the kitchen door burst open and Ben stormed in, with Danny hot on his heels.

"Just what do you think you are playing at?" he shouted at Melissa.

Kirsty stared at him, her mouth dropping open.

You shouldn't be here, thought Issy. It didn't work.

"I have been halfway round Sussex because of your childish little ploy and I'm going out and . . ."

"Are you, darling?" said his mother in delight. "Who with?"

"A gurrr . . ." Danny shut his mouth as Ben threw him a savage glance.

"Friends," said Ben firmly. "And because of her," he stabbed a finger towards his sister, "I'm going to be late."

Kirsty was still staring at him, not a muscle in her face moving.

I knew it, thought Issy miserably. I knew it.

"What are you on about, Ben dear?" asked his mother.

"Melissa told Danny to invent some stupid story about you and a broken-down car," he said. "Just because she was having some dippy friend . . ."

His mother glared.

Ben stopped and looked at Kirsty as if seeing her for the first time. "Oh, er – sorry. It's not you – it's her. I'll go and change."

And blushing furiously he slammed the door and stamped upstairs.

"What have you been up to, Melissa?" asked her mother.

"Later," hissed Issy.

"I'd better be going," said Kirsty, looking from one to the other and pushing back her chair.

"But dear, you haven't had any dessert yet," protested Fay.

Kirsty hesitated, obviously feeling uncomfortable because of the atmosphere.

"I'm sorry, I'm really, really sorry," said Melissa. "I didn't mean him to be here. I knew you'd be upset – that's why I told Danny to keep him away."

Kirsty frowned.

Mrs Bailey sat down and looked at her daughter. "Explain."

It was not a request, it was an order.

"I knew Kirsty would be upset at seeing Ben, so I paid Danny to tell him that you had broken down in the car so that we'd have finished tea and be upstairs before he got back. But it went wrong," she concluded miserably.

"But why would Kirsty not want to see Ben?" frowned her mother. "He's not Dracula, he's only your brother, for goodness sake . . . oh!"

Light dawned first on Fay's face and then on Kirsty's.

"You thought that because of Tom, I'd be upset at seeing your family?" Kirsty asked incredulously.

Melissa nodded. "I felt guilty that I'd got my brothers and you hadn't," she admitted. "I mean – Ben's the same age as Tom would have been and . . ." Her voice faltered.

Kirsty hugged her. "That was so sweet," she said. "But it isn't like that, honestly. I'm really glad I've met Ben. There's only one thing I'm annoyed with you about."

Melissa looked concerned. "What?"

"Not telling me sooner that you had a brother who is a total dish!"

". . . and once, when we were little, Tom built this pirate ship at the bottom of the garden, out of old bits of wood and stuff and then made me walk the plank over the stream. When I fell off he ran to the house saying I'd drowned and gave my mum a real heart attack!"

Kirsty giggled and took another jam tart from the plate. Melissa had gone to answer the telephone and Mrs Bailey was plying Kirsty with questions about her brother.

"You know, this is the first time I've been able to talk about the naughty things he did," she said. "Mum and Dad go on about him as if he was some sort of saint and God knows . . . oh gosh. Sorry."

Mrs Bailey laughed. "Don't apologise," she said. "God does know. He knows that Tom could be a pain at times and do silly things. And since it doesn't make a bit of difference to him it shouldn't make any to us. I guess your parents are still grieving so much that they think they have to put Tom on a pedestal."

Kirsty nodded thoughtfully. "You know, you're really normal – for a clergy person, I mean," she said and then gulped. "Oh sorry – that came out all wrong too."

"I'm delighted to hear you think I'm normal," said Fay. "Although my kids might disagree with you."

"About what?" Melissa crashed through the door.

"Kirsty thinks I'm normal," said her mum.

"She'll learn," said Melissa.

CHAPTER FOURTEEN
EXCUSES, EXCUSES . . .

MELISSA LAY IN BED STARING at the ceiling. She couldn't get to sleep. She kept thinking about Matt Carter and wishing she hadn't let Kirsty say all that stuff about the party. He must think she was really sad and anyway, he was bound to have a girlfriend at college. College! He went to Cortlesham, which meant that Ben was bound to know him. Why hadn't she thought of that before? She could raise the subject in a roundabout sort of way and get her brother to find out what he thought of her! That way, if he thought she was a nerd, she could start playing it cool before he did. She would corner Ben first thing tomorrow before she went to London.

It would be so cool to be in London again. She felt a bit guilty about lying to Kirsty about having visitors – but then it wouldn't have been fair to invite her along and then for Ellie and Tara to be rotten to her. So really she was doing the best thing all round.

Consoling herself with that thought, she pulled the duvet up round her neck and closed her eyes.

Hugo threw back the duvet and quietly padded through to the kitchenette. Pouring himself a glass of milk, he sat down at the table and put his head in his hands.

It was wrong. He knew that. Delightful, exciting,

unexpected, exhilarating – but wrong. He should never have started it. And now he knew beyond all shadow of a doubt he had to finish it.

How could he have been so stupid? Suppose Fay had found out? What would it have done to her? And the kids – what would they have thought of him? He'd always tried to be a role model for the boys and Issy, someone they could look up to and respect. If they had found out . . .

But no one was going to find out because after tonight, there was going to be nothing to discover. He would tell her, gently but firmly, that it had been wonderful but that it was over.

Downing the last drop of milk, he put the glass into the sink and walked back through the open-plan sitting-room to the bedroom.

He would tell her. He had to. Just as soon as she woke up.

Ben couldn't sleep. He was too wound up. He was normal after all. He had kissed her and she hadn't laughed. She had kissed him back, she had run her fingers through his hair and his skin had tingled, just like the book said it would.

Only then she didn't want to stop. She had started sliding her hands inside his shirt and half of him had felt in heaven and the other half had wanted to say, "Let's go for a pizza." And the other half won. She had seemed a bit surprised but he didn't want things to happen so fast; for now he just wanted to enjoy being with her, and get used to the fact that his kisses were OK, and maybe to work a bit on his chat-up technique and then – well, the rest could happen later. There was no rush.

But then what if she got bored? What if she dumped him for someone like Matt Carter, who obviously knew just what to do and had no inhibitions about doing it?

He thumped his fist into his pillow and rolled over on to his stomach. He'd do better next time; he'd chill out more.

He'd do whatever it took. He couldn't bear to lose her.

"Ben! Can I come in? It's me, Issy."

Ben thrust *Supercool With The Opposite Sex* under the covers and swung his legs out of bed. After his horrible dream in which Matt Carter had kissed Vicki in the middle of a giant pizza, he really needed to get to grips with chapter four, 'Fighting off the Competition'.

The door opened and his sister burst in.

She was wearing a giant paper-clip earring in one ear and a scarlet pencil in the other. She looked like a stationery advert.

"Ben, do you know Matt Carter?"

"Oh sure!" spat Ben.

"I mean, is he a real mate of yours?"

"Get real? Me a mate of Matt Carter's? Oh please."

Melissa frowned. "What's wrong with him?"

"Nothing, I suppose, if you like people who are really up themselves," snarled Ben, knowing he was being unfair but still smarting from the effects of the bad dream. "Anyway, what's it to you?"

Issy sat on the end of the bed and inspected her newly varnished yellow fingernails.

"I don't suppose," she began, twiddling the huge imitation garnet ring on her right hand, "that you could sort of find out what he thinks of me?"

Ben peered at her. "Do you know him?"

"We've met," said Issy loftily. "I just thought – well, he is quite nice."

Ben was about to give her his views on Matt when a thought crossed his mind. If he could get him interested in Issy, he might just stop eyeing up Vicki.

"OK," he said, "I'll see what I can do. Not that I think he's your sort."

"You just do the asking," ordered Melissa. "I'll be the judge of what's good for me."

CHAPTER FIFTEEN
PLEASE DON'T LET IT BE TRUE...

"THAT WAS THE BEST MORNING ever!" Ellie Balfour said for the fourth time, as she chewed on a wedge of pizza on the canal-side terrace of Pasta Go-Go overlooking Camden Lock. "This velvet top will look so sophis. with my black hipsters. They don't have anything like it in Cortlesham."

Issy grinned. Her friends had been well impressed, not just with the dress shop but with Camden Market, where Tara had bought armfuls of beaded bangles and a pair of wicked suede boots.

"So where next?" demanded Tara, downing the final drop of cola.

"Fancy a makeover?" asked Issy. "Face It Folks do them for free if you buy just one thing. It's just round the corner."

"Ace!" said Ellie. "I've always fancied the silent, sultry look."

"Silent? You?" teased Tara.

"So let's pay and get going," suggested Melissa, thrusting her hand into her leopardskin bucket bag. "Oh no!"

"What?" chorused the other two.

"My purse – it's gone!" She peered into the bag with mounting horror.

"It can't have," reasoned Ellie, grabbing the bag. "You're right – it's not there."

"I know that!" said Issy, close to tears. "It had all my money in it – and my train ticket home and everything. What shall I do?"

Ellie frowned. "You could go to the police," she said.

"Or phone your parents," suggested Tara.

"I know!" exclaimed Issy. "Dad stayed up in London last night. His flat's only a ten-minute walk from here."

"Will he still be there?"

"Probably not," said Issy. "But the guys on security know me from when we helped Dad move in – maybe they'd lend me a tenner and then Dad could pay them back."

"Brill!" said Tara.

"Let's go then," said Issy.

"You go," said Ellie. "We'll look round the shops till you get back. We can't waste serious spending time."

"Oh," said Melissa. "OK then. But you'll have to pay my share of lunch for now."

"Only for now," said Ellie sharply.

Issy nodded. She was still feeling a bit sick from the shock of losing her money and wished the others would go with her. But they were already discussing which shop to go to first.

"Meet you back here in half an hour?"

She picked up her bag and walked across the street. She prayed her dad would still be at the flat.

If he was there everything would be all right.

"Was that the 11.20 from Victoria?" Fay Bailey poked her head through the enquiry window at Cortlesham station. She was sure Hugo had said that he would catch that train but there was no sign of him.

"Yes, love," said the ticket clerk. "Next one's due in at 1.45."

Terrific, thought Fay, stomping back to the car. I can't hang around any longer, I've got to get Danny to riding.

Where is he? she thought, slamming the car into reverse gear. Why didn't he phone me on the mobile to say he would be late?

In the pit of her stomach there was a worrying niggle.

What if something had happened to him?

What if he was ill? He'd be alone in the flat and no one would know.

She pulled up at the nearest phone box and jumped out.

She'd call. At least that way she'd know if he had left.

Please be there, Issy prayed silently. Please, please be there.

The lift clanked to a halt on the fifth floor and she stepped out. As she turned left into the narrow corridor she noticed that the door to her father's flat was wide open and from inside she heard a familiar voice.

"I have to go, I'm late as it is. Really, this is the only way to do it."

Dad! Thank you, God. Thank you, thank you, thank you.

It sounded like he was on the phone to some boring client. She sped down the corridor and peered through the open door.

"Dad! Da . . . oh!"

She stopped dead.

Standing just inside the doorway was her father.

And in his arms was a woman with long fair hair and a black skirt with a slit up the side.

And he was kissing her.

Not a peck on the cheek. A real, passionate, lingering kiss.

Issy's throat went dry.

The kiss went on. Then her father suddenly pulled back and began pushing the woman away. She clung to him.

"Don't," she sobbed.

Issy's legs wouldn't move.

The woman ran her fingers through her dad's hair.

"Oh, Jo, Jo." Her father's voice was cracking.

Issy's heart was about to explode in her chest.

On the table, the telephone began to shrill.

Her father looked up, pushing the woman away from him.

And then he saw Issy.

Issy ran. She didn't bother to wait for the lift, she ignored her father's calls to her, begging her to wait.

She clattered down the stairs, gulping in air, and ran across the foyer and through the door, oblivious to the astonished look on the face of the man at the security desk.

Only when she had rounded the corner did she stop, leaning against a shop window and panting for breath.

Her father was having an affair. He couldn't be. There had to be some other explanation.

But he was. You don't kiss people like that if you're just good friends.

Her dad wouldn't do that. Other people's fathers might go off the rails but not her dad.

She wanted to cry but the tears wouldn't come. She didn't know what to do.

The others would be waiting. She'd have to pretend everything was hunky-dory.

And somehow she'd have to find some money for the fare home.

Suddenly she wished Kirsty was there. She wouldn't have to keep up a front for Kirsty. But she couldn't let Ellie and Tara know – they'd have it round the whole school by Monday lunch-time.

She began walking back to the canal.

She fixed a smile on her face and scrutinised her reflection in a shop window to make sure she looked normal.

She took a deep breath and walked to where the others were waiting.

"Hi!" Ellie spotted her and waved. "Guess what?"

"What?"

"The waiter found your purse – you must have dropped it when you went to the salad bar."

She handed Issy the red purse. "Did you catch your dad? Have you got loads more cash?"

Whether it was relief at finding her money, or the mention of her father's name, she didn't know.

But to her horror, right there in the middle of the street, Melissa burst into tears.

Fay turned the car into the driveway and peered at the figure standing on the doorstep. It was Kirsty and she didn't look very happy.

"Kirsty! How are you?"

Kirsty turned round and Fay could see that she had been crying.

"Oh, hi Mrs Bailey," she said. "I'm really sorry to call when you've got visitors and everything . . ."

"We don't have visitors, dear," said Fay, puzzled. "But I'm afraid Melissa's not in – she's up in town with her friends. What a shame you weren't allowed to go!"

Kirsty stared at her. "I could have done," she said abruptly. "I suggested we spent today together but Issy said you had company."

"And Issy told me that your parents forbade you to . . . oh, never mind. Come on in. Is something wrong?"

"No – yes – I . . ."

Kirsty burst into tears.

Hugo hailed a taxi and jumped into the back seat.

"Victoria, as fast as possible, please," he said.

Leaning back in the seat he closed his eyes.

Just think calmly, he told himself. All you have to do is explain to Melissa that you were comforting a young member of staff who – who had just failed her qualifying exams. Yes, that would be good – Issy was already worrying about GCSEs; she'd identify with that.

Who are you kidding? he asked himself crossly. She saw us. She saw how it was.

He'd have to try a different tack. Tell her it was just a minute's aberration – that nothing had happened. He'd have to make sure she believed him – if she told Ben, or Fay . . .

It didn't bear thinking about.

Why had he been such a fool?

Why had he allowed himself that one long, final kiss? Why hadn't he just ignored Jo's tears and told her to leave?

Why?

"But what's happened?" Ellie asked Melissa for the third time.

"I can't tell you," she said. "I've just got to go home."

"What – now?"

Issy nodded.

"Oh great, spoil the day, why don't you?" snapped Tara.

"You can stay," said Issy. "You can still go shopping. Look, if you just get the Northern Line down to Tottenham Court Road, there's that cool record shop I was telling you about."

"But why can't you stay?" urged Ellie.

"Oh – family probs, my dad told me about," said Issy. "I have to get home."

". . . so you see, it just shows that I'm not good enough for either of them, Mum or Dad," sobbed Kirsty, twisting a sheet of paper towel in her fingers.

"No, no," soothed Mrs Bailey, "it doesn't show that at all. It shows that your parents are beginning to think about moving on . . ."

"Oh yes? And replacing Tom with another baby?"

Mrs Bailey took her hand. "You said your mum was only talking about the possibility of having another baby," she said. "She talked to you about it, remember? She asked you how you would feel. Does that suggest that she doesn't care about you?"

Kirsty sniffed but said nothing.

"Grief is something that everyone who loses a person they love has to go through," explained Fay. "People deal with it in different ways; for your mum, it meant visiting the cemetery and thinking about all the wonderful things that Tom did – but don't you see? She now realises what joy having children has given her. That's why she is thinking about having another."

Kirsty stared. "Why can't I be enough?"

Mrs Bailey smiled. "I don't think you'd want to be," she said. "Oh, it sounds terrific, doesn't it? But if your mum centred her whole life round you, all her worries, hopes, ambitions, fears – well, it would make your life pretty hard, wouldn't it? You said it was tough enough having your dad nagging you to achieve all the time."

Kirsty nodded. "You make things so clear," she said. "I wish . . ."

"What?"

"I wish my mum and dad could talk to you – you could tell them how I feel."

Mrs Bailey smiled. "My door is always open, the church is always open," she said. "But they have to decide they want to talk. I can't make them."

Kirsty nodded. "Why did Issy lie to me?" she asked suddenly. "Why did she tell me you had visitors?"

"I don't know," said Fay grimly. "But I have every intention of finding out."

"Mum? It's me. I'm at Victoria. Can you meet me at Cortlesham? I know. I'll explain later. Oh Mum. Please be there, please."

"I'm on my way, darling."

Hugo leaned against the phone cubicle in Victoria

station. "Chapter of accidents – personnel problems, you just wouldn't believe. I could have done with your people skills, I can tell you."

That was good. He'd laid the foundations nicely.

"See you in about an hour. Sorry, darling – Issy's what? Didn't catch that – announcements on the loudspeaker. Look, my money is running out. Bye!"

It'll be all right. It will. Please, God, make it all right and I'll never be so foolish again.

I'll have to tell her, thought Melissa, staring unseeingly out of the train window. But I can't. She'll be devastated.

But if I don't, and Dad goes on seeing this hateful woman, they'll get divorced and then what will happen to all of us?

Perhaps I should talk to Dad first. But then he'll fob me off with some story and I'll never know whether he's stopped.

Maybe Ben will know what to do. Except he won't believe me – he'll say I'm overreacting because in his eyes Dad can do no wrong.

And I can't talk to Danny – he's too young.

Kirsty! I could phone Kirsty and see what she thinks. Except that I'd have to admit I was in London and then she'd be upset and . . . oh, what do I do?

Mum says that truth always pays in the end and that once things are out in the open they can be sorted. Mum says God always sides with the righteous.

Only he didn't do much for her, did he?

He didn't make Dad behave.

But then maybe it wasn't Dad's fault. Maybe that woman seduced him and he was powerless to fight back.

And if I tell Mum, she'll forgive him, won't she? Because that's what she's always on about. Forgiving people their trespasses and all that.

And besides, we're supposed to stamp out evil.

And that woman is definitely evil.

I'll tell Mum.

I think.

"Mum! Mum!" Melissa yanked open the car door and threw herself into her mother's arms.

"Oh Mum, I do love you!" she said and burst into tears.

"Darling, whatever is it? Have you been hurt? No one's done anything to you, have they?"

Issy shook her head. "No – it's . . . it's Dad – I lost my purse, you see and . . ."

"Oh darling! How wretched for you. Did . . ."

". . . so I went to Dad's flat to borrow some cash and – and . . ."

She couldn't go on. She couldn't tell her.

"And he'd left? He should be on this train – oh yes, look, here he comes. You must have been on the same train as him without knowing it."

Melissa looked out of the front window of the car in horror. Her dad was striding across the carpark towards them. When he spotted Issy, his face paled for an instant before he fixed a bright smile on his lips, opened the rear door and clambered in.

"Fay darling!" He leaned forward, kissed his wife on the back of the neck and turned to kiss Issy.

She flung her head to one side. "Don't!" she hissed.

"Poor Issy lost her purse," said Fay conversationally. "She went to your flat . . ."

"He knows," said Melissa clenching her fists.

Her mother slid the car into reverse and peered over her right shoulder. "So you did manage to catch him? I thought you must have because you got home in one piece. That's good!"

"Oh, I caught him all right!" said Issy with a catch in her voice. "I saw . . ."

Hugo touched Issy on the shoulder. "Everything's just fine now," he said and then wondered what had made him utter such a stupid remark.

"Well, it may be fine for you!" snapped Issy. "It's not so bloody wonderful for us!"

"Melissa! Don't use words like that! What is going on?"

"Ask Dad."

"Hugo?"

"Just a little misunderstanding," said Hugo. "Let's get home and talk about it later."

"Oh, later?" Melissa shouted. "What, when you've thought up a good excuse?"

"Issy, what you saw wasn't . . ."

"What she saw? What are you on about?" Mrs

Bailey switched off the ignition. "Will someone tell me what is going on."

"Dad's having an affair, that's what's going on!" sobbed Melissa. "And I saw it all!"

She shouldn't have yelled it out like that. She should have done it all differently.

Her mother's face drained of colour. Her knuckles whitened as they gripped the steering wheel.

"Hugo?"

Melissa turned, waiting to hear what her father had to say.

Hugo took a deep breath. "I am not having an affair," he said and his voice was shaking. "Issy's got it all wrong . . ."

"Oh, so you go around kissing every woman you know and running your hands all over them and . . ."

Issy couldn't go on. She was sobbing too hard.

"I know it looked bad, I know what you think, but I was just telling Jo . . ."

He stopped.

Melissa saw that his eyes were filled with tears. She had never seen her father cry.

If she had kept quiet, he wouldn't be crying now.

But was he crying because he hurt Mum? Or because of that woman?

"Say something, Mum," sobbed Issy.

"I think," her mother said, breathing deeply, "that we should all go home and talk this through calmly."

She switched on the engine and drove in silence on to the main road.

No one spoke.

As her mother pulled up at the traffic-lights, a solitary tear splashed on to the gear lever.

Issy felt as if the end of the world had come.

CHAPTER SIXTEEN
TROUBLES NEVER COME SINGLY

"DAD AND I NEED TO TALK," said Fay, putting the key into the front door lock. Melissa saw that her hand was shaking.

"Issy, I want you to walk over to the riding-school and fetch Danny," she said. "You've got plenty of time – he doesn't finish until four thirty."

"But, Mum, can't I stay and . . ."

"Issy, just go!" Her father's voice was husky with emotion. "Please."

She didn't want to go. What if her mum threw him out? What if he asked her for a divorce?

"You will be OK, won't you?" She looked nervously at her mother.

"We'll be fine," she said. "Just give us some time alone, OK?"

Melissa went through to the kitchen where Barnaby was snoring under the table, blissfully unaware that their lives had just been turned upside-down.

"Walk," said Issy without enthusiasm.

Instantly Barnaby was awake, leaping to his feet and knocking over a pine stool in his haste to get to the back door.

From the sitting-room Issy could hear the sound of raised voices.

". . . and to think I believed that you were working!"

She clipped Barnaby's lead on to his collar and opened the back door. Suddenly she wanted to be as far away from Church Hill as she could get.

". . . and I suppose if Melissa hadn't turned up on the scene, this – this *affair* would just have carried on," sobbed Fay.

Hugo put an arm round her. Fay shrugged him away.

"No – honestly, I had told Joanna that it had to stop. I mean, it had hardly started – truly it hadn't. I knew it was wrong. I was saying goodbye to her when . . ."

"Oh, so saying goodbye means kissing and fondling her in front of our fourteen-year-old daughter, does it?"

Hugo sighed. "I would give anything for that not to have happened," he admitted. "I had no idea she was in London, never mind coming to the flat – you might have told me."

The instant he said it, he knew it was a mistake.

"So – I should have told you so that you could have arranged your rendezvous elsewhere, is that it?"

"No, I didn't mean – oh, this is ridiculous!"

"No, what is ridiculous is the thought of you – a middle-aged man – getting involved with a girl young enough to be your daughter!" shouted Fay. "Didn't you give a thought to us? Your family? And what about my reputation in the village?"

As soon as she had said that, she knew that she too had made a mistake.

"So now we get to the point!" snapped Hugo. "It's not our relationship that really matters, is it? It's just your job that counts. Well doesn't it occur to you that just possibly it was your wretched job that drove me to look at someone else in the first place?"

Fay stared at him.

He stared back.

"I'm sorry," he began. "I shouldn't have said that."

"No – wait," whispered Fay. "I thought – I mean, you said you were behind me taking this post. You knew what it entailed . . ."

Hugo sighed. "I know, I know – strangers ringing the bell at all hours, you going off to meetings and everyone seeing me as nothing more than Mr Curate."

For a long moment Fay was silent. "You've always been far more than that to me," she whispered.

She took a step nearer. "Do you love me?"

Hugo smiled. "You know I do – I adore you," he said. "I guess Jo just flattered my ego, made me feel important, made me even wonder if I could do something worthwhile like her . . ."

"I think," said Fay, "we have a lot to talk through."

"So do you forgive me?"

"I don't know. You'll have to give me time. I honestly don't know if I can."

She'll have to forgive him, Melissa thought as she ambled up the lane to Fox Hollow Equestrian Centre. It's in her job description. She did a whole sermon once about turning the other cheek, which had seemed like a pretty dumb idea at the time. In fact they'd had a long argument over Sunday lunch because Ben said an eye for an eye and a tooth for a tooth made much more sense and Mum said it wasn't as simple as that. Not that it felt, right now, as if anything would ever be simple again.

"Here, Barnaby!" she called as they walked through the gate of the Fox Hollow Equestrian Centre. She clipped the lead on to his collar and began walking towards the field where a group of kids were hurtling towards a row of painted fences on plump little ponies looking just like designs for a Thelwell Christmas card. She spotted Danny, elbows and legs going like the sails on an overactive windmill as he turned his pony towards the fences.

I wish I was his age again, she thought. When I was eleven I thought Dad was perfect too. Now I know better.

She watched as her brother cantered at full speed and popped over some red and white rails, a row of upturned oil drums and a small brush fence. He was good. She was impressed.

The fences were being put to a higher level and

Danny was about to take his second turn.

"Look, Barnaby!" said Issy. "See Daniel?"

Barnaby looked. And liked what he saw.

With a quick wrench, he pulled the lead from Melissa's slackened grip and galloped full-tilt towards the ponies – just as Danny was heading for the first hurdle.

Danny jumped it and cantered towards the next fence.

Barnaby put on an extra spurt and followed, tongue lolling.

The instructor shouted something incomprehensible.

"Barnaby!" shouted Issy. "Come back!"

Barnaby took no notice but shot towards the second jump, overtaking Danny's grey pony.

Barnaby jumped the second jump.

Danny's pony saw the dog, whinnied, swerved and stopped.

Danny didn't. He flew over the pony's head and landed on the ground on the far side of the fence.

"Danny!" Issy screamed and rushed over to where the instructor was already bending over Danny's prone form.

"That's my brother!" she gasped, dropping down on one knee beside him. "Is he all right?"

The instructor looked up. "I think," she said, "that we had better call an ambulance."

He looked so little. He looked so white. And his arm was sticking out at a funny angle.

Barnaby, shut firmly in the tack room, peered mournfully through the window.

"Where is the ambulance?" Issy said for the third time in three minutes. "Why don't they come?"

She walked to the gate and peered down the road. "Please, God, make them come."

A figure on a bicycle was pedalling furiously towards her. It was Ben.

"Ben!" she shouted. "Come quickly! There's been an accident."

"Oh no you don't!" he said. "You've tried that trick once too often. I want to know what's going on."

"It's not a trick. Danny . . ."

"Shut it, Issy! What's going on at home? I got back from town and they were both shouting and Mum was crying."

For an instant, with the shock of Danny's fall, all thoughts of her parents had slipped from Melissa's mind. They returned with a jolt.

"And then they just told me to come and make sure you and Danny were OK. What's . . ."

"I'm OK, but Danny's not!" shouted Issy, determined to make him listen. "He fell off his pony."

"He's done that heaps of times," began her brother.

"They've called an ambulance," said Issy, tears filling her eyes. "He isn't moving. And it's all my fault."

In the distance a siren began wailing. It was coming closer.

The ambulance rounded the corner.

"Now do you believe me?" cried Issy.

Ben said nothing. He was already sprinting through the gate, calling his brother's name.

"The phone's ringing," said Fay.

"Leave it," said Hugo.

"I can't," protested Fay. "Someone might be dying."

She picked up the receiver. "Fay Bailey speaking. Oh Ben – what? Oh my . . . Cortlesham Hospital. Of course. But is he OK? I'm coming. I'm on my way."

She slammed the receiver down and ran to the front door.

"What's happened?" asked Hugo, following her.

"It's Danny," she said. "He's had a fall. He's unconscious."

"I'll get the car," said Hugo. And paused. "Unless," he said softly, "you don't want me to come?"

"Of course," said Fay. "Danny will need you there."

The waiting area of the Accident and Emergency room was packed.

Danny had been taken into a cubicle and Ben and Issy had been banished to wait in a corner where there were a few hard chairs and a table with five-year-old magazines.

"He'll be all right," Ben assured Issy. "He woke up in the ambulance. He was asking for Mum and Dad. At least this will stop them arguing."

Issy swallowed. He'd have to know sooner or later.

"For a bit," she muttered.

"You know something," said Ben, giving her a penetrating look. "Tell me."

Issy told him.

"I don't believe you!" Ben's face was white and tense. "Dad would never do a thing like that. Are you sure you're not exaggerating?"

"For the last time, I know what I saw!" snapped Issy. "But he said it was nothing and it was all over, and Mum's bound to forgive him. I mean, he was wrong and everything but . . ."

"You don't know that it was Dad's fault!" retorted Ben, jumping to his feet and causing several of the other out-patients to give him curious glances. "That woman – it was probably all down to her. She probably came on so strong that he had no choice . . ."

"Oh don't give me that!" argued Issy. "He's a grown man, he didn't have to snog . . ."

"Shut up! I don't want to hear about it! I bet there's a perfectly simple explanation and Dad . . ."

"Sssh!" Issy nudged him. "They're coming."

Their parents hurried towards them.

"Where is he?"

"What's he done?"

"Have you seen the doctor?"

A nurse stuck her head around the curtain of a nearby cubicle. "Mr and Mrs Bailey? Come through. You can see Danny now."

"It was a simply enormous jump, wasn't it, Issy?"

Two hours later, Danny was sitting up in bed in the children's ward, proudly displaying a plastered arm and reliving his experiences with a little extra embellishment for each time of telling.

"I'm not very pleased that they let you tackle such a big fence," said his mother anxiously. "You obviously aren't ready for that yet."

"I am so!" said Danny indignantly. "If Barnaby hadn't joined in, Buttons wouldn't have . . ."

"What's Barnaby got to do with it?"

It may well be time, thought Issy, to tell them the full story.

Issy kicked off her shoes and lay on the bed. It had been a horrid evening. They had all hated leaving Danny in the children's ward, although it had to be said that he seemed more upset at missing The Simpsons than at waving goodbye to his family.

All the way back to Fox Hollow, where Barnaby had remained locked in the tack room by the irate proprietor, her father had gone on and on about how irresponsible she had been, allowing her dog to endanger the public safety. By the time they turned into the drive, it had been agreed that Issy would enrol Barnaby into obedience school at once.

"It's time you thought about the consequences of your actions, Melissa," he had said. "Having a pet is a big responsibility and . . ."

"Having a family's a responsibility too – not, it

seems, that it bothered you!" she had stormed, partly out of guilt at what had happened to Danny and partly because she couldn't stand her father's hypocrisy.

"That's enough, Melissa!" her mother had said tightly.

"Dad's right," countered Ben. "That dog's a menace."

She hadn't spoken since then. She had eaten her supper in silence, almost choking on every mouthful. How could they be like that? Mum shutting her up and Ben taking Dad's side after all that he'd done. Ben and her father had even gone off for a walk together after supper, as if nothing had happened. And Mum had shut herself in the study to finish her sermon for the following morning. When Issy asked what was happening, her mother had simply said that life had to go on and hadn't she got homework to do?

She wondered idly how Tara and Ellie had got on in London. It seemed a lifetime ago that they were joking around in Glad Rags. She wished she'd never gone to London. That way she would never have found out.

She was about to undress when there was a tap on the door.

"Issy? Are you still awake?"

Her mum came into the room. She looked tired and drawn and the whites of her eyes were pink.

Suddenly Issy forgot all her grudges and threw herself into her mum's arms. "Mum, I'm sorry about Barnaby and Danny and everything, and I'm sorry that I let on about Dad, only I didn't know what to do and . . ."

Her mother hugged her back. "It's OK," she said. "I guess Danny's fall frightened you enough to ensure that you take more care in future. And as for Dad – well, it would have come out some time, the truth always does. What I want to know is why you lied."

Melissa's mouth dropped open. What was she on about? "I didn't lie, I did see him . . ."

"Not about your father," said her mother acerbically. "Why did you lie to your friend?"

"What do you mean?"

"You told Kirsty we had visitors; you told me that her parents wouldn't let her go to London."

Ah, thought Issy.

"She came round today and it all came out," said her mother. "I think she was pretty hurt."

"Well I can't do everything with her!" said Issy defensively. "I mean, Ellie and Tara think Kirsty's a real saddo and . . ."

"And do you think that?"

"No, of course not – I really like her. But you don't know what it's like."

"So tell me."

"Well, it took ages to get in with Ellie and that lot – I mean, they're really cool and everyone wants to be in their crowd. No way would they include me in stuff if Kirsty was tagging along all the time."

"So you're finishing with her as a mate, are you?"

"I never said that," protested Issy. "I really like her, I'll just go around with her when . . ."

"When you've nothing better to do, is that it?"

Issy said nothing. Put like that she felt pretty mean.

Her mum took her hand. "I know you've been keen to make lots of friends, love," she said. "But friendship is a commitment – it's not just something you can pick up and put down as it suits you."

She smoothed a crease in the duvet cover. "Kirsty's had a tough time," she said. "And when people are going through a bad patch, they need to know someone is there for them. Like you do right now."

"But it's going to be all right, isn't it?" asked Issy. "I mean, you and Dad . . ."

"We're both going to try very hard," acknowledged her mother.

"Both?" said Issy. "But you don't have to do anything – it's Dad."

Her mother shook her head. "It's rarely that simple," she said. "Dad feels left out, he thinks that the church means more to me than he does."

"And does it?"

Her mother shook her head. "My job – my faith – they mean so much," she said. "But so does my family. It's not a competition. There's room for them all. What I have to do is make sure that I show Dad that."

"So it's going to be all right?"

"I hope so," said her mum. "But these things don't mend overnight, any more than Kirsty can get over her brother's death in just a few months. We all have to put on brave faces and carry on with our lives –

you and Kirsty at school, me in the parish, Dad at the office – but we all need to know that there is somebody we *don't* have to pretend with. Kirsty thought you were that person. Now I don't think she is quite so sure."

Melissa nodded slowly. She thought about how Ellie and Tara hadn't really given a toss when she burst into tears in front of them. They hadn't picked up the phone to find out how she was. They probably hadn't given her another thought – and all because shopping was more exciting. She didn't want Kirsty to think she was like that.

"Do you think," Issy asked her mum, "that it is too late to phone Kirsty?"

Ben shoved his hands in his jacket pockets and turned into Spinney Rise. It was gone ten o'clock but he wasn't ready to go home yet. He had to get things clear in his head after this awful day.

He felt as if he had been walking for ever. First of all, he and his dad had taken Barnaby and strolled all the way to the Titchcombe cross-roads and back, and Hugo had told him about this Joanna woman and how he had never meant things to get out of hand.

"I love your mother," he had insisted over and over again. "But I guess I succumbed to the flattery of a pretty woman. I suppose that happens to you all the time!" He had given his son a playful nudge in the arm.

"For God's sake, Dad!" Ben had shouted. "This isn't a joke. You're a married man, not a college kid – you can't just go around having a fling because some woman gives you the come-on!"

An image of Vicki floated unbidden into his mind and he gave a little shudder as he recalled the way she had clung to him the previous evening, nibbling his earlobe and asking him if he thought she was pretty. He remembered how he had felt – but he was seventeen. Dad was fifty-one and should know better.

"And just what would have happened if Issy hadn't shown up?" he had demanded. "Would you have gone on seeing her behind Mum's back?"

"No, of course not," his father had insisted. "I knew it was wrong. I had already decided to put an end to it. Mum and I are going to work hard and sort it all out – so can we please talk about something else?"

Only somehow neither of them could think of anything else to talk about and Hugo had gone home, leaving Ben alone with Barnaby. And his thoughts.

It wasn't Dad's fault, he decided. This Joanna woman was obviously totally unprincipled and had been out to seduce him from the start. She probably didn't even love him; she was after his money and his know-how. That would be it. Poor Dad – he was so trusting that he probably didn't realise what was happening until it was too late. He had been used.

There probably were a lot of women like that. For all he knew, Vicki could be one of them – maybe she was only coming on strong to him because she wanted him to do her computing assignments and get her an A grade. When he was with her he felt all sorts of emotions he had never felt before and some of them were pretty overwhelming. Scary even. Perhaps that was what had happened to Dad.

But it would be OK now. Mum wouldn't throw him out – curates had to be seen to be pillars of the community.

A thought suddenly struck him. He had better make sure that Issy didn't go blabbing about all this to any of her mates. It would never do for it to get round the parish. No one must know. Not ever.

"Come on, dog," he said. "Home time." He quickened his step, determined to speak to his sister before she went to bed.

Barnaby loped on ahead at the end of the extending lead. Ben was just in the process of unravelling him from a bus stop, round which Barnaby had hurled himself in pursuit of an empty crisp packet, when a familiar voice made him jump.

"If it isn't the horrible hound!"

He turned to see Matt Carter emerging from the late-night supermarket carrying a four-pack of lager. Matt walked over and stooped to pat Barnaby, who promptly planted a muddy paw on his jeans.

"Barnaby! Down!" Ben commanded. "Sorry, Matt – he's a perfect pain!"

Matt looked at him in surprise.

"Ben! What are you doing with this mongrel? Where's the angry ant?"

"The what?"

"The girl it belongs to – short kid, red hair, temper to match – right little raver!"

Ben bristled. "The 'right little raver', as you put it, happens to be my sister," he said.

Matt's eyes widened and his cheeks flushed. "Melissa? Your sister? Oh gee – sorry! She is sort of cute though."

Despite himself, Ben smiled. "Actually, she thinks you're pretty OK too," he said.

To his utter astonishment, Matt's face flooded with colour and he became hugely interested in the small print on the lager cans.

"In fact," said Ben, "I guess you're in there if you want to be."

"Nah," Matt said hastily. "Too young for me – I go for the more womanly woman, if you take my meaning! That friend of hers, for starters! Anyway, must go – see you around."

Ben watched him thoughtfully as he sped off down Priory Lane. He was glad Matt didn't fancy Issy because she deserved better. But his sister would be mortified. He'd have to think of a gentle way to tell her.

But first he had to make sure she kept her mouth shut about things that really mattered.

CHAPTER SEVENTEEN
FINDING THE RIGHT WORDS

5 Church Hill
Mannings Green

Dear Kirsty
I tried phoning you last night,
but there was no reply. I guess
you were at your gran's and I
haven't got her number.
Anyway, what I am writing
for is to say I am really sorry
for lying to you. It was a horrid
thing to do – I guess I thought
Tara and Ellie were mega cool
and they're not. The whole
day went wrong and the only
person I wanted to talk to was
you. And now you probably
won't want to be friends
with me and I don't blame you.
Everything's going wrong...

Melissa paused and crossed out the last sentence. Ben

said that no one must know about Dad and she supposed he was right. After all, people expected church families to be as pure as the driven snow and if the vicar found out, Mum might lose her job.

Not that she was likely to get the chance to tell Kirsty. She would probably never speak to her again.

Anyway, I still want to be your friend and if you give me a second chance I promise to do it better this time.
See you,
love Issy

It didn't say everything she wanted to say but it was a start. She shoved the note into her pocket and ran downstairs. If Kirsty was in church she would give it to her then; if not, she'd put it through her gran's letterbox.

She just hoped it would do the trick.

Fay stood in the choirstalls, trying to concentrate on the words of the first hymn. She couldn't believe that it was only one week since she had stood in this very spot feeling so happy, so certain that everything in her life was going the right way. Now all she felt was a great, hollow emptiness and a lump deep in her throat.

It wasn't fair. She had given up a lot to do this job and now God had rewarded her by throwing all this in her face. Not, of course, that she expected rewards – but she didn't expect a whole load of grief either.

She looked across to the gap in the front row of the choir where Danny usually stood. At least he was blissfully unaware of what had happened. And they must keep it that way. He was too young to cope.

Not that coping was easy, however old you were. Issy kept telling her every five minutes that she had to forgive Dad because that's what the *Bible* said, which was rich coming from a kid who only a week ago had said religion was a farce.

And Hugo? Hugo said he loved her; Hugo said it would never happen again. But could she believe him? Until now she would never have questioned a word he said but suddenly she wasn't so sure.

In a few minutes she would have to climb the pulpit steps and preach a sermon. There were people out there who needed words of wisdom. People like Kirsty's parents, sitting nervously at the very back with their daughter, looking as if they wanted to be anywhere but there. But how could she, whose own life was in a mess, tell anyone else how they should be living theirs? She didn't have any wisdom left. She didn't know what she was going to say – none of the words she had been working on came out right. How could they, when it was as if everything she had ever believed in had been called into question?

Well no. Not everything. Some things were unshakeable. She knew, even on the days when she couldn't get it right, that God meant her to do this job. And if that was true, then surely he would give her the strength to do it. She knew too, that he had given her three great kids and a husband who loved her. He hadn't promised her a life without problems; he had promised her to be there when she needed him. All she had to do was ask. Well, now she was asking.

The choir rose to a crescendo.

"Here I am, Lord.
Is it I, Lord?
I have heard You calling in the night.
I will go, Lord, if You lead me,
I will hold Your people in my heart."

"Here goes," murmured the Reverend Bailey, as she moved in front of the chancel steps.

"It's easy, isn't it?" she said, leaning forward from the pulpit and surveying the congregation. "When everything is going well, we say how wonderful God is, and we come to church and hurl a few pence into the collection plate and go home, sure that we have done our bit to ensure that life continues the way we want it to."

The congregation coughed. They weren't so stupid that they didn't see a punch line when it was coming. Ben stopped picking the skin round his thumb and looked up at his mother.

"But when things get tough – well, it's very different then, isn't it? *'Why has God done this to me?'* we cry. *'How can he say he loves us and then let something like this happen?'* "

She was conscious of a sharp intake of breath from several parts of the church. She spotted Issy, face cupped in her hands, staring at her anxiously.

"Familiar, isn't it?" Fay challenged. "We all do it. You do it. I do it. Oh yes – I do it. Just because I wear this," she touched her clerical collar, "doesn't mean I don't throw the odd saucepan lid and stamp my foot occasionally."

The congregation chuckled with relief. She wasn't going to go all pompous on them.

"Just imagine a life without problems or crises. A life in which no one we loved ever hurt us . . ."

She paused and took a deep breath. ". . . no one we loved ever died, and we never experienced pain or anxiety. Sounds great, doesn't it?"

The congregation murmured.

"But what would happen? We would stagnate. Pain and tragedy and conflict are actually channels through which we grow. And we can do it. How?

Because of love. Our love for one another, God's love for us."

She paused. She saw Kirsty's parents watching her intently. She saw Hugo blowing his nose surreptitiously. In her mind's eye she saw Danny giggling from a hospital bed.

"Love is what matters, God is what sees us through. Whatever else you give up on in life, don't give up on God. And never, ever give up on love."

My mum is amazing, thought Issy. That was so brilliant. It's like good always comes out of the bad bits. And better still, it means she's sticking with Dad.

Yes! thought Ben. She's come through. It's going to be all right.

Thank you, God, whispered Hugo, dabbing furtively at his eyes with a pocket handkerchief. Help me to show her how much I care.

"Kirsty," said Kirsty's mum softly. "Thanks ever so for making us come along."

"Cool, isn't it?" Kirsty balanced two glasses of orange squash and nodded towards a poster for The C-Zone, Fay's new club for teenagers.

"The coffee looked putrid so I got you orange – is that OK?"

Issy swallowed. "Yes, great – thanks. Er – did you read the note?"

Kirsty nodded. "It was really nice of you to write it,"

she said. "I was pretty cheesed off but then I got to thinking that actually you were probably meant to be out of the way."

Issy drew back. "What do you mean?"

"Well," said Kirsty, "if you had been at home when I called, I'd never have dared to sit and talk to your mum like I did. She is amazing – she made so much sense. I guess she told you about this baby idea?"

Issy shook her head. "Mum never repeats anything that people tell her," she said. "That's why our house is always full of people opening their hearts and eating our ginger biscuits. What baby?"

Kirsty laughed. "I'll tell you later," she said.

"So we are still friends?"

"Of course – provided you do one small thing for me."

"Anything," said Issy. "I owe you one."

"That's what I thought!" agreed Kirsty.

"So what is it?"

"Come to the youth group with me this week."

Melissa groaned. "Do I have to?"

"Uh-huh."

"You drive a hard bargain."

CHAPTER EIGHTEEN
BROTHERLY LOVE

"AND THE DOCTOR SAID I WAS incredibubl – incredi – very, very brave!" pronounced Danny, who had pride of place on the sofa where he was stabbing a plate of chicken with his good hand.

"I think," said Hugo, carving himself another slice, "there are quite a few brave people around here."

He looked at his wife and she gave him a gentle smile.

"I've got to feed Humphrey," said Danny. "And clean his cage – only I can't because of my arm."

"I'll do it," said Issy reluctantly. "After all, it's my fault you broke it. I never really said sorry, Danny."

"It's OK," said Danny cheerfully. "Although I am thinking of suing for compensation. How does maths homework for two weeks sound?"

"You little . . ." She was interrupted by the shrilling of the phone.

"I'll get it!" cried Ben, leaping up and spilling gravy all over the table. "It'll be for me."

"It's never for you," protested Issy but Ben had gone.

"Probably it's his girlfriend," said Danny matter-of-factly and then clamped his hand to his mouth. "Oh, whoops!"

"Ben's got a girlfriend?" His mother dropped her fork in surprise. "Really?"

Danny nodded. "But you're not supposed to know. Why aren't you supposed to know, do you think? It's not a bad thing to have a girlfriend, is it?"

There was a momentary silence.

"No," said Fay after a minute. "Not when you're seventeen."

"Hi, Ben? Vicki!"

I'll tell her now, he thought. It's all getting too complicated.

"Ben, I was wondering. Could we meet? This afternoon? There's something I want to talk about."

Just say no. Say you've got homework. Say your brother's just come out of hospital.

"OK then. Where?"

Why couldn't it stay just like this? Walking through Lipton Woods with Vicki, Barnaby being ridiculous and making them laugh – it was so normal. So peaceful.

"Can we stop for a minute?" Vicki looked up at him pleadingly.

Here we go, thought Ben. This time I've got to get it right.

"I don't know how to put this so I'm just going to say it," said Vicki in a rush. "I really, really like going out with you and I'd really like it to go on just the way it is."

She paused. "I've never met a guy like you before," she said shyly. "You make me feel special."

Ben glowed. But any minute now . . .

"And you seem to like me even without all the – well, you know."

Ben looked at her. Could she be saying what he thought she was saying? "Without what?"

"Sex and stuff," she said. "I mean, don't get me wrong. I really fancy you."

"You do?"

"Of course – who wouldn't?"

Ben thought he might die of joy.

"But I'm not ready for anything else," she finished. "I've tried to make myself want to – well, you know, go further, but I just can't. Do you mind?"

"Mind? Of course I don't. I just thought that you were the one who wanted . . . oh never mind."

She smiled. "I thought if I didn't come on strong, you'd go off with someone else."

Ben laughed out loud. "And I thought that if I didn't prove I was stud of the year, you'd take up with Matt Carter."

"Matt? Get real. He's terrified of girls. He talks like he's so cool but underneath he's ever so shy."

"Really?" Ben looked thoughtful. So that was why Matt had blushed so much when Ben told him that Issy was keen. And to think he had imagined that Matt was supercool.

"It's a pity really," said Vicki, "because he's a nice guy underneath. Anyway, let's not talk about him. Can you put up with having me for a girlfriend?"

"Oh yes," said Ben. "No trouble at all."

"You never said you had a girlfriend!" Melissa did not believe in beating about the bush.

"Well, I do," said Ben equably. Now that he knew where he stood, he wanted the entire universe to know that he and Vicki were an item.

"I'm really pleased," said Issy, giving him a hug. "Mind you, I'll have to vet her and make sure she's good enough for you."

Ben grinned. "You let me get on with my own love life, thank you and just concentrate on sorting yourself out."

Issy's eyes lit up. "Did you talk to Matt? Did he say he fancied me? Is he going to ask me out?"

"No," said Ben.

"Oh," said Issy.

"But I'm sure that pretty soon someone far nicer will."

CHAPTER NINETEEN
THE WAY AHEAD

"IT'S FUNNY HOW THINGS TURN OUT, isn't it?" mused Melissa, one evening a couple of months later, as she and Kirsty lay sprawled on her bedroom floor, reading back copies of *Heaven Sent*.

"I mean, if I hadn't rebelled against the oh-so-sacred uniform code that day, you and I might never have got together . . ."

". . . and I would never have tried to get you and Matt together . . ."

". . . and you would never have met my mum and dragged me along to The C-Zone . . ."

". . . and the course of our entire lives could have been totally different!" concluded Kirsty.

And if I hadn't lost my purse and found out about Dad, I could still pretend he was totally perfect and Mum wouldn't have been unhappy and Danny wouldn't have broken his arm and life would be wonderful, thought Issy, casting her eye over the problem page.

Only life wasn't wonderful, not all the time. And problems didn't vanish overnight. Her parents were making a real effort, but she knew her mother listened at the door if her father was on the phone to someone she didn't know; Melissa had seen how she flicked through the mail each morning and frowned at any envelope with unknown handwriting.

Her dad had been pretty put-out when the church authorities refused to let him knock down walls and complained that it was an outmoded institution with no flair or panache – but at least he had got his own way over the redecoration and was going overboard on stripping floorboards and sandblasting fireplaces.

It had been hard keeping all the problems to herself

and pretending to her mates that everything was great. So many times she had wanted to tell Kirsty about what had really happened. On the Monday after Danny's accident, Ellie had gone round telling everyone about how Melissa Bailey abandoned them in central London like a real drama queen and wouldn't tell them what was wrong – and Melissa had pretended to Kirsty that she'd had a migraine. She knew Kirsty didn't believe a word of it.

But she couldn't drop her dad in it. OK, so he'd been a complete idiot but he was her dad and she did love him. And Ben was right; if it got round the village, Mum's life would be hell, and she couldn't do that to her. So she just kept it to herself.

"And," continued Kirsty, interrupting her thoughts, "if it hadn't been for me, you wouldn't be in love!"

Issy grinned. She had a point. She hadn't wanted to go to Ellie's party after all the things she had been saying, but Kirsty had had other ideas.

"I bet you the only reason she's been on and on about Matt going is because she wants to get off with him herself!" she had said to Issy the night before the bash. "You can't cry off now – it'll be a hoot!"

Even Matt, on being told the full story, seemed to think it would be a laugh. "Go on, AA, play along with it – just for fun!" he had urged.

He called her AA all the time now – it was short for Angry Ant.

So she'd gone.

And when Issy had swanned in, beaming, with Matt hard on her heels, Ellie had gone all coy and simpered and fluttered her eyelashes and told Matt she'd been dying to meet him because skateboarders turned her on.

And when Kirsty had appeared at the door, wearing a very short slip dress with shoestring straps and a wicked lilac feather boa, and waltzed up to Matt and planted a kiss on his cheek, Ellie's eyes had popped out on stalks.

"What are you doing here?" she had demanded.

"Kirsty's with me," Matt had said. "She's my girlfriend."

It hadn't been how Issy would have imagined it two weeks earlier but she had to admit it had been a laugh.

Of course, none of that mattered at all now. At first she had been a bit miffed that Matt wanted to know whether Kirsty was going to the party before saying yes and even more miffed when Kirsty had admitted that Matt had gone round to her gran's house while she was there and asked her to get Issy to lay off.

"It's not that he doesn't like you," she had said over and over again. "He thinks you're really sassy."

"But not sassy enough to take out!" Issy had muttered.

"Actually – well, he told me not to say anything . . . but you're my mate and . . ."

"Don't tell me I've got B.O.?" Melissa had cried.

"No, silly! Matt says he can't go out with you because you're Ben's sister."

"So?"

"Matt thinks he's useless with girls and you'll tell Ben he's rubbish and then Ben will spread it all round college, because your brother is sex on legs!"

Issy had frowned. "You have to be joking," she exclaimed.

There was a long pause while Kirsty nibbled her thumbnail.

"Actually," she said, "Matt said he would go to the party."

"Great!"

"With me. Only because he says he has to start somewhere," she had added kindly. "Do you hate me?"

If it had been Ellie or Tara, the answer would have been a definite yes.

"Of course I don't," Issy had said. "You're my best friend."

"Come on!" Issy said to Kirsty now, throwing her magazine on to the bed and jumping up. "We'll be late for The C-Zone!"

"That's rich coming from the person who vowed she would never set foot inside a youth club!" giggled Kirsty.

"Well, I want to support my mum . . ." began Issy, unzipping her make-up bag.

"Very noble," said Kirsty. "And the fact that Flick

Thomas will be there has absolutely nothing to do with it?"

"We're just friends," said Issy, who had decided to keep quiet about the long and rather intimate snogging session behind Ellie's father's Jaguar the night of the party. "Nothing heavy. OK – I'm ready."

She was about to open the door when it swung back in her face and Danny hurtled in.

"Quick!" he cried. "I've lost Geraldine!"

"Who's Geraldine?" asked Kirsty.

Issy grabbed his collar. "Don't tell me you've got another rat!" she shouted.

"Oh no," said Danny.

"Thank heavens for that," said his sister.

"Geraldine's a snake."

"What?" gasped the two girls in disbelief.

"I'm snake-sitting for Luke, while his tonsils come out. Only she got out."

From the hallway below there came a piercing scream.

"I think," he said, "Mum might just have found her."

Issy sank down on the bed. "Brothers are such a pain!" she said. "Oh – sorry, I . . ."

"Don't start that again!" smiled Kirsty. "It's OK – besides, I agree. Tom had an ant farm when we were little and it was no fun when they escaped, I can tell you! I've told Mum that this time it has to be a sister."

"She's pregnant?"

Kirsty nodded. "Really into the bootees and bottle-versus-breast bit," she said.

"Do you mind?"

"Mind? I'm delighted. We've talked more about feelings and fears in these past two months than ever before. They've even stopped going on about my grades – perhaps they're counting on the baby to be the family genius!"

Issy laughed.

"But you know the best bit?" said Kirsty.

"No," said Issy.

"We're getting to be a real close family again. I mean, I know you've never had it any other way. But, believe me, it's such a good feeling."

Issy nodded slowly.

"Yes," she said. "Yes, it is, isn't it?"

Also in The Girls *series by Rosie Rushton*:

SOPHIE

Sophie is smart and sassy. She has brains, she has money. But she is plagued with a mother who's obsessed about becoming rich and meeting the 'right' people. And her love life is a mess – due, she's sure, to the fact that she blushes like crazy. Partying is OK, but Sophie wants a life that's real.

Tony is real. He isn't cool and he isn't fit. He's just a mate, which is wonderful, as Sophie doesn't have to act trendy or sexy when she's with him.

When her dad comes home from doing good works in Africa, Sophie is delighted. At least he is in touch with what really matters. But then he gets her involved in helping the homeless, and Sophie is confronted with more reality than she can cope with.

Just when it's all getting too heavy, Sophie discovers another kind of real, when something happens that makes her go weak at the knees for the first time ever . . .

Also in The Girls *series by Rosie Rushton*:

OLIVIA

How much more can Olivia cope with? Her dad has gone off to live with the Wretched Rosalie - and shows no sign of coming home. Her boyfriend has dumped her and she just knows it's because she has fat thighs and freckles. Her arty mother has decided to take a zany lodger - and is very definitely being led astray by her. And to make matters worse, her best friend Poppy, who had the answers to everything, has moved to a new school.

But when drop dead gorgeous Ryan starts seriously chatting her up and her dad announces that he is coming back to Leehampton, Livi thinks that life is on the up. *But that is when the real problems start!*

Also in The Girls *series by Rosie Rushton*:

POPPY

Poppy has it all. She's pretty, she's popular, she has a model family and boys queuing up to take her out. And because she's also very nice, she just loves sorting out the traumas of her less fortunate friends – as befits one who intends to become the country's youngest agony aunt.

Whether it's organising the sponsored dance for Comic Relief, dragging her headmaster into the nineties or comforting her best friend, Livi, over the disappearance of her boyfriend into the arms of Mia Fazackerly, Poppy can handle anything . . .

Or can she? When Poppy's secure environment begins to crumble around her, her abilities to cope are really tested.

Teenage angst and problems handled with wit and empathy" The Bookseller, Pick of Children's Books

Also available from Piccadilly Press by Rosie Rushton:

THE LEEHAMPTON QUARTET

Just Don't Make a Scene, Mum!

This is the first in the tremendously popular Leehampton trilogy about five teenagers and their very embarrassing parents.

". . . cool and diverting comedy . . ." – The Times

I Think I'll Just Curl Up and Die

They thought their parents couldn't get any more embarrassing – then they get worse!

"Light-hearted but sure-footed, she juggles the humour, heartache and heavy breathing with an easy balance of wit and sympathy . . ." – Joanna Carey of the Guardian

How Could You Do This to Me, Mum?

Chelsea, Jemma, Sumitha, Jon and Laura are back again in another hilarious book!

". . . it will be read to death . . . it's wonderful" – Books for Keeps

Also available from Piccadilly Press, by Kathryn Lamb:

HELP! MY FAMILY IS DRIVING ME CRAZY!
A Survival Guide for Teenagers

"An essential survival guide for all those teenagers with embarrassing/annoying parents and siblings." - The Children's Bookseller

HELP! MY SOCIAL LIFE IS A MESS!
A Survival Guide for Teenagers

"Are your friends boring? Are you too busy swotting to party? Is the opposite sex completely alien to you? Are you becoming your parents? Then get help fast. This essential guide is full of practical solutions to improve your popularity and spice up your social life." - Word Up

HELP! LET ME OUT OF HERE!
Your Guide to Taking the Stress Out of School

". . . suggests destressing as one way of surviving secondary school. Hugely entertaining yet perceptive and practical, this guide will make clear . . . just how much of a cool school dude (you) want to be. Highly recommendable." The Bookseller

If you would like more information about books available from Piccadilly Press and how to order them, please contact us at:

Piccadilly Press Ltd
5 Castle Road
London
NW1 8PR

Fax: 0171 267 4493